SHAM ROCK

A DECLAN McGUINNESS MYSTERY

TOM CADOGAN

Fulton Books, Inc.
Meadville, PA

Published by Fulton Books 2021

ISBN 978-1-64952-563-5 (paperback)
ISBN 978-1-64952-564-2 (digital)

Printed in the United States of America

To my dear friend, Cormac Hayes:
When you're over fifty, there's only six months to a year.

FOREWORD

I t's seldom easy for killers to get rid of a body. Bodies have a way of turning up, if not in reality, at least in nightmares. For thousands of years, killers favored the classic method of bag, drag, and dump. If one lived near water, and a boat was handy, disposal was made simpler. For the bog men of ancient Ireland, the remains of victims could be dragged to a seemingly permanent hiding place, where vengeful relatives or others could not easily find them. But perhaps to the chagrin of the perpetrators, bodies in bog water (humic acid) were preserved indefinitely. A centuries-old body recently found in an Irish bog had a retina scanned through the gel of an eye, revealing incipient major-organ failure in a man of forty-two years—a mature age for the time of his death. Had the man's skull not been cleaved with an axe, he would soon have died of something else. So with the advance of forensics, it's even more difficult to hide bodies. Disposal must be carefully planned, lest the door be opened to unwelcome discovery.

Ireland, of course, being an ancient land, is full of bodies: hidden, turned to dust, or absorbed into the lexicon of history. Most visitors to Ireland enjoy discovering the images of lush green hills and pastures, character-laden skies, and medieval, mossy ruins. But while they seldom think about it, the bodies are never far away, occasionally demanding attention. "How could you leave such a beautiful place?" a noted emigrant was once asked. "Too much of the past is buried under those images," he said. "Besides, you can't eat scenery."

The Irish know that the struggle to keep the postcard picture intact means giving up some benefits of a modern European community. Many thousands in the Irish diaspora who escaped the various struggles of more difficult times return to Ireland, hoping to find the images unchanged. They know, however, that change is inevitable despite the ongoing cultural and economic effort to keep the landscape clear of innovations. One way or another, superhighways, water towers, electrical grids, and other such industrial paraphernalia are kept out of reach. Besides, digging around could turn up those bodies.

Preserve, recycle, and sustain could be considered Irish watchwords. In the face of pressures to modernize, the Irish have succeeded in installing some of Europe's most advanced elements of change while at the same time retaining the inherent, quintessential charm of the island. So now they have sleek, little electric cars racing between charging stations on narrow, rural roads. Passive homes can be comfortably maintained and operated with just a few solar panels, even though the fireplace and the turf bucket are never far away. And the triple-pane windows overlook vistas that have changed little since the time of Cromwell.

The Irish have apparently been willing to pay the price for their efforts. All renovations are bureaucratically monitored and licensed—the old versus the new; safety and convenience versus risk and complexity. Ireland is right to stall the march of progress if life-affirming culture is threatened so long as the better path to the future is not trampled out of existence. This part of Irish character is always on display for visitors to the "Auld Sod." It is the essence of their existence and the plinth for their poetry and art.

Ireland is as close to the Arctic as Newfoundland, but lies beneath the swirl of atmosphere warmed by the constant drift of the Gulf Stream. This air spawns rains and clouds, broken by brilliant sun, followed by more rains and clouds. The Irish climate is a continuous challenge and inspiration. In the midst of summer, the mornings can be clear and bright, like a spring day with all the promise of growth to come, followed by a cool and cloudy evening reminiscent of a fall day and the beginning of a new school year. In the same spot, it can be warm in the sun and frosty in the shade, the constant presence of the yin and yang of life itself; the constant reminder that you're not that far from the ice age when you're walking the fields in Cavan.

In Ireland the air is always clean and clear and wistful. The lush grasses eventually turn into some of the best cream and butter in the world, but it's the food for the soul that will infuse every fiber of your being. There is just something about the place and the people that will leave a lasting impression—one to be cherished—both the scenery and the bodies of the past.

The story you're about to read is set in Ireland and a world sometime in the future. Fiction is about a possible, even implausible, reflection of reality. For Inspector Declan McGuinness of the Gardai, and some of the other characters in this tale, the past is always prologue no matter where reality takes them. They live in a future world but are never disconnected from those ancients in the bog, who controlled fate as surely as the twists and turns in their DNA did.

CHAPTER 1

Sometime, decades in the future, the whole climate-change thing started to unravel. That is, events started to stabilize; sea-level rises were greatly reduced or abated, polar ice held fast, and storms moderated. Areas in severe drought got more rainfall, while flooding occurred less frequently. The changes were gradual and apparently connected to a reduction in global greenhouse gases, primarily carbon dioxide, by one means or another. Scientific journals and news reports started to grab headline attention, and parts-per-million measurements became a routine topic of conversation.

Some were still not convinced that changes in human activity had altered the course of events. Of course, the devastation caused by rising sea levels, mass people and animal migration, and other spin-off effects were apparent everywhere around the world, but this could be attributed to cyclic influences. What rises must fall. Many accepted that reversals in fortune were inevitable and closer at hand than the millions of years it would take for changes in the carbon cycle.

There was, however, one major factor, which turned all heads skyward and changed the thinking of many of the unconvinced. Observations and measurements from the Lunar Base Complex had put things in perspective. The word from space made it incontrovertible. There was no doubt that changes in climate activity could be traced to specific manmade initiatives witnessed from space. Great swaths of ocean and patches of desert were gobbling up the carbon dioxide faster than anyone had predicted. The absorption and sequestration of gases was discernible, and accelerants were really working to lower the concentrations of carbon dioxide in the atmosphere.

Ireland was no exception to the detriments of climate change, and the southern coast had lost much of the waterfront by the future time things started to reverse. By then, Kinsale, a small town at the mouth of the River Bandon, had a population of 6,290. The town, once considered a microcosm of the nation as a whole, was now undergoing a rebirth with construction and renovation everywhere in sight. Still, the new face—such as it was—did not detract from the medieval, picturesque qualities of the old town despite the waterline markings visible on many buildings along the waterfront.

The technology of robo vehicles and drones helped the inhabitants to circulate without the requirement for major disruptions to the street grid. Advanced solar power generation and the advent of nanocapacitor storage batteries virtually eliminated the need to string unsightly power lines. Next-generation digital communication made towers unnecessary. If one could ascribe a modicum of prescience to the Irish, it could be said that they neglected to upgrade all the old systems, knowing that new technology would make it all redundant. One could, but one would be wrong. Lack of resources was the real reason, as it was for most people around the globe. Still, the practicality of the Irish couldn't be ignored.

It was onto this turf that Bob Foley clambered, making his way around the robo bus to get his one travel bag from the storage compartment. It had been a white-knuckler of a ride from Cork Airport, as roadside brush scraped the sides of the speeding, driverless bus. Actually, it wasn't much better than his first bus ride from Cork, when there was a driver who seemed to have a heavier gas foot than this "robot." At least it wasn't raining like the first time.

Many of the roads in Ireland could still be considered primitive if you discounted the pastoral appeal of meandering, shoulder-poor lanes. Since the whole nation had a population half that of New York City, an interlacing of ribbons of concrete was hardly a desirable or necessary option. Someday teleportation would be a real thing, and the roads could be left to the scampering of voles and wandering hikers. In the interim, the rut-riding wheels of the robo bus were a necessary forbearance, though a fascination to Bob Foley.

Today, in fact, was a beautiful sunlit day in June, the type shown in most of the tourist circulars, distracting the unwary from the more-typical Irish gloom. Bob made his way over to the boat basin and saw once again that the return of low tide had exposed acres of dank and fishy-smelling mud—less than before, but still attention-grabbing. The return of good boating memories, when sailors had to beat the tide, brought a smile to his face.

On the other side of the street, the Upton Hotel was busy with tourists, carefully skirting the scaffolding, walkways, and platforms hastily erected for remodeling in the wake of the improving climate events. He thought about getting something to eat in the new cafeteria but changed his mind when he glanced at his phone and checked the time. He was to meet with his son, Jimmy, in an hour and had to get to the Rock, his ancestral home. This would entail a lengthy walk over to Lower Road then down Scilly Walk, dragging his bag all the way.

As an American expatriate in his fifties, Bob was a dual citizen who sported his passports proudly. It was even better now that Ireland was part of the Republic of Europe, the sensible but seemingly impossible eventuality of the old EU. There was finally one European Defense Force with English as the *lingua franca*. NATO became an anachronism, and the United States finally had an ally that was its equal in all respects, with a militia even more culturally diverse than its own.

Bob was a former US Navy commander who lost his wife to cancer shortly after he retired. He traveled extensively in Europe and saw how the mixing of cultures in the EDF had accelerated the cementing of a common purpose throughout the continent, eclipsing most of the national bickering and paranoia common for years. Many of the young who didn't serve in the military opted for a stint in the International Peace Corps, with even better results for improving the global village. Things weren't perfect, but cynicism was dealt a healthy blow.

As a pensioner, Bob was pursuing his art hobbies and restoring his ancestral home in Kinsale. Back in EU days, the Irish government had instituted tax advantages for artists which were continued in the ER. This gave him some extra cash, which with his US investments helped his construction budget. He wasn't much of a builder, but with his son Jim's help, he managed to convince the Cork County

Council that remodeling a coastal home in the face of changing sea levels was a serious, achievable goal.

Bob had engaged an architect to see him through the project. The architect spent half his time in London, England, and had a curious antediluvian way of speaking. Bob and Jim called him Lord Blarney because he provided progress reports with a profusion of indecipherable flourishes, which translated to little in the way of intelligent discourse. Fortunately, the contractor, Stitch Hegerty, could understand him and his scratchy drawings. Blarney's sketches, though, when turned into CAD printouts, were impressive. They managed to favorably convince the council and any neighbors curious about what Bob and Jim were doing.

His foster father, JJ, who built the house forty years earlier following the death of his wife, christened the place "Sham Rock." JJ came up with this sobriquet as a tribute to Otis Sham, who sold him the property. Eventually, the family just came to calling it the "Rock." This, too, was appropriate since the house was reached from Scilly Walk by passing through a short tunnel drilled through a near-vertical shale wall. As you entered the tunnel through a heavy door, you would need to climb several meters up a series of limestone steps to then exit onto an asphalt driveway. There was the feeling that you entered the side of a small mountain. With the heavy brush, neither the driveway nor the house could be seen from Scilly Walk.

JJ Foley was, among other things, a fairly good artist. He never remarried, and his life became filled with chasing his career and educating and raising Bob, to whom he gave his name. In many ways, Bob saw his project to rehabilitate the Rock as a tribute to JJ, who died in his nineties and for whom he had an abiding love and many pleasant memories.

Bob finally made it to the entrance on Scilly Walk, tired and hungry. He traced his finger around the large brass shamrock mounted on the oak door. Surprisingly, it had recently been polished. He punched in the code on the security pad over the handle: S-H-A-M-R-O-C-K 7426 7625. At the other side of the driveway, which connected to Higher Road, an iron gate with similar keypad fronted the property.

A small gray Toyota biofuel/electric hybrid was parked on the driveway. It wasn't Jim's car, and it couldn't have belonged to Donal Riordan, his maintenance man. Donal drove an old Ford pickup. Anyway, it was still a little early for Jim who was working today. At least this was the reason Jim gave for not meeting him; though he worked in the city, minutes from the airport. If the Rock had a visitor, he or she would be known soon enough.

CHAPTER 2

The Rock was a heavily insulated brick and frame structure, covered with a gable roof of concrete tiles. The original chimney and fireplace had been removed in the rebuilding process, and a solar-powered heat pump and storage battery provided the necessary power and heat. A biofuel-powered electric generator was added for emergency backup, but aside from maintenance checks, it was never run or needed. The house was set at the top of the promontory in a wooded area. Frequent trimming of overgrowth was required to ensure clearance for proper solar reception.

A large, triple-paned window at the front of the house looked out on Bandon River, and though part of the stony beach could be seen, Scilly Walk was not visible. Bob had plans to install a video camera over the door on the Walk, but it was not an immediate priority. A Wi-Fi connection enabled him to monitor the heating, electric, and ventilation from the States, and this was enough for the time being.

Bob found the front door open, and the chime as he entered alerted someone inside.

"Be with you in a minute." A tall woman in her twenties bounced into view from a ground-floor bathroom. She wore faded jeans and a cotton blouse with rolled-up sleeves. She also had rubber gloves and carried a scrub brush. "Oh my gosh! You must be Mr. Foley. I hoped to be finished before you arrived. I'm Caitlin McGuinness, Jimmy's friend."

"Caitlin. Yes. Jim mentioned you, and you're even prettier than the picture he put in my head. But he forgot to mention he was putting you to work while he gallivanted in Cork."

They both laughed and exchanged small talk. He told her to call him "Bob as he wrestled his bag into the main bedroom. It was

14

clear from cursory inspection that she had done yeoman's service in getting the place ready. She even discovered his stash of Jameson and had it set out in a carafe with three gleaming Waterford glasses.

"I can make tea in a jiffy, Bob, if you prefer, and you can try one of my strawberry scones," she offered.

Bob was enjoying her company and the scones when a car pulled into the driveway. Jim Foley was dressed in fatigues and dismounted his robo Volvo with a small black bag. He grinned broadly when he spotted Caitlin and his father.

"Sorry I'm late, folk. I had to do water-sampling and other work in the River Lee today. Busy, busy."

As a marine biologist working for a US company, Ocean Technologies Inc., Jim Foley lived in Cork year-round. He expected to be in his current assignment for two years, but he hadn't reckoned on meeting Caitlin, a teacher and climate-change activist who grew up in Dublin.

Bob and Jim switched to Jameson after two cups of tea, toasted Caitlin, and engaged in animated conversation about the progress of the remaining work on the Rock, Bob's trip over from the States, and the difficulties of finding a good computer guy in Kinsale.

The three eventually gravitated over to a new pub in Scilly, or rather an old pub with new owners. They lit into a meal of mussels in wine sauce, with chunks of fresh bread and Irish butter, washed down with mugs of ale. By the late afternoon, they were enjoying the rosy glow when Caitlin said she had to get back to Cork, excused herself, gave Jim a kiss, thanked Bob for the meal, and left in her Toyota.

The pub owner switched a large wall television to an RTE news channel, and a nattily dressed anchor popped into view. He looked like he had combed his hair with a can of shoe polish and seemed a tad breathless.

"We're here today on the beautiful yacht, *Fancy Fran*, moored in Kinsale harbor, for an interview with owner, billionaire CEO of Mercer Enterprises, Conrad Mercer, and his lovely wife, Frances."

The camera angle changed to show the couple seated in overstuffed deck chairs against a background of glass, stainless steel, and highly polished wood. Gulls circled the harbor, adding contrast to scudding white clouds.

"That's the guy I'm supposed to see next week," said Jim, turning to his father.

"You're kidding. He owns waterfront property all over the world. They say he made a killing by buying up submerged land abandoned because of rising tides. How the hell did he know any of it would be dry again?" Bob swigged his ale in disbelief.

"A lot of it is still underwater," said Jim. "So how does he keep his backers in tow? That's my question."

"What do you have to see him about? Are you going to make him an offer for his yacht?" snickered Bob.

"Not this time. Mercer knows that OT has several patents for kelp with a ravenous appetite for carbon dioxide. What the plants don't digest, they convert to a limestone ash. He expressed interest in large scale projects but didn't say specifically what he had in mind." Jim turned his attention to the ongoing television interview.

Con Mercer was smoothing his white jacket and responding to the interviewer's question, "Of course, there were no guarantees. Like most estate agents, I had to do a lot of schmoozing with owners, other agents, local entrepreneurs, and politicians. They wondered what I knew that they didn't. Of course, I was taking a gamble, but I was pretty confident that Mother Earth would reward my optimism."

The news anchor leaned forward and said, "Most people have come to the conclusion, given what's happened, that the scientists were correct. Carbon dioxide added to the atmosphere by human activity caused the warming, the ice melt, and the eventual sea rise. But scientists also said the gas would be around for thousands of years. How did you plan to deal with that?"

A sudden gust of air ruffled Mercer's white hair as he responded, "So we have two challenges here if we ever want to get the sea back to where it belongs. First, we take steps to slow the tons of carbon we're putting into the air. Second, we do things to dissipate the gas already there. The global community has done a good job, at long last, on the first item. It's the second point that you're really asking about, so let me put something out there." Now Mercer was leaning out.

"Methane is a greenhouse gas ten times more powerful as a warmer than carbon dioxide. But methane dissipates in a few years. What we're doing is making carbon dioxide more like methane by using a few chemical tricks. I'm one of several companies that's partnering with various governments. What I'm saying, if RTE won't censor me, is that cow farts are better for us than petrol exhaust because they won't hang around for the millennia."

The news anchor blanched a little, smiled, and said, "And how is that working out, Mr. Mercer—the second part, that is?"

"Things are improving, as you can see by observing the seaside in Kinsale. I'd like to see a lot faster movement and more investment, but we have some ideas and plans in the works. I'm not at liberty to discuss all of this, but stay tuned. In the meanwhile, everyone is invited to visit our hospitality table aboard the *Fancy Fran*. We have a launch for their convenience, departing the boat basin on the hour."

Listening in, Bob said he'd like to take Mercer up on his offer, but he was already bushed from his long trip from the States and needed to get back to the Rock. Jim would go back with him and return to Cork in the morning.

Back at the Rock, Jim wanted to show his father the new work accomplished by the contractor since Bob's last visit. Unfortunately, there wasn't much to see. The contractor, Stitch Hegarty, was very good at coming up with creative excuses for his lack of productivity. Stitch was given this name after he sewed up a gash in his brother's leg following a climbing accident. His brother subsequently died from infection, but the doctor was impressed by the quality of the stitch work. This was Stitch's problem. He was a perfectionist, seemingly never reaching closure. His brother used to keep him in line, but sadly, there was no one to do that now.

"Take a look at the handrail along the steps going down to the ground floor." Jim traced his fingers along the intricate Celtic design cut into the oak uprights. "I don't know why we needed this, Dad, but it is beautiful."

"It should be. He charged me 2,500 euros extra for it," Bob said.

CHAPTER 3

Declan McGuinness rubbed his considerable chin. As a decorated Gardai inspector, he felt obligated to bring the Kinsale Red Green murder case to a swift conclusion. He was troubled, though, that for a whole month no leads had been followed. The file had been sent from Cork District, to which he was detailed from Dublin Met, and he carefully reviewed it during the train ride from Dublin to Cork's Parnell Station.

Red Green was the file name for Scarlet Kelly, the nude girl in her twenties found on the beach near Scilly Walk. She was stabbed to death, and her body had been in Bandon River for about a week. A fisherman from Kinsale found the body, but there was no record of any witness statements in the file. This was a serious oversight by the Kinsale Gardai.

According to the medical examiner, there was DNA in the vaginal area, but it was degraded to the point of uselessness. The fingerprints were on file because the girl had been arrested three years earlier on a drug offense. A toxicology screen was run, but nothing was found. There was no indication of the drugs she was taking when she was arrested three years ago. The murder weapon wasn't found, but the examiner thought it might have been a serrated kitchen knife, about twenty centimeters long, judging by the wound. Also, rope fibers were found on the right ankle.

The boys at Cork District couldn't add anything except to say that they had no additional information on any interviews conducted with area locals. Also, the girl's father in Waterford appeared to be the only living relative. He hadn't seen or talked to his daughter since she left home at sixteen and didn't know where she worked or what she did. The district gave Declan a robo car for his use while on the case, for which he was grateful. Maybe he could get to see his daughter, Caitlin, and catch up. The unfortunate Mr. Kelly in Waterford would never be able to do this with his daughter.

He telephoned Caitlin and got her answering machine. He would try again later after he got a room in a motel and a bite to eat.

Eventually, they did connect, and Caitlin wanted to cook a meal for her dad. Declan explained that he had already eaten, and that meeting in a pub would give them more time to talk. He would take notes, he said, so that Caitlin's mother, Honey, would get all the right answers to her many questions. Caitlin laughed, agreed, and gave directions to Declan.

Declan hadn't seen his daughter for a month but knew that her latest boyfriend was an American scientist for whom she had serious feelings. At first, Declan was concerned the guy would eventually go back to the States, leaving Caitlin to pick up the pieces of a wham-bam relationship. He felt better when he learned that the guy was the son of Bob Foley, an old friend that he went to school with at Ohio State University. He knew Bob was retired USN, planning to move to his father's old place in Kinsale. Getting to see his daughter and reconnect with Bob would be bright spots on this otherwise depressing Red Green tableau. Good. Jim Foley might become a great son-in-law, and he and Honey wouldn't have to worry about Caitlin. He looked forward to seeing Bob Foley again and eventually meeting Bob's son, Jim.

Caitlin had good things to say about the Foleys, especially about Jim's projects with Ocean Technology (OT) greenhouse-gas sequestration and coral-reef protection. Declan was pleased, but only half listening. He looked at Caitlin but kept visualizing the file photos of Scarlet Kelly. He couldn't imagine how any father could deal with such a devastating loss.

"I worry about you, Caitlin. What I see of the human condition is not encouraging, and I'm not talking about climate change."

"How ironic, Da. You and Mom couldn't wait to get me out on my own, and now you're having empty-nest regrets." She laughed.

The following morning Declan had breakfast at a cafe near his motel. He arrived in Kinsale a couple hours later, in time for a second cup of tea at the Gardai Station, which he savored before getting down to business.

Sergeant Pat Twomey's ruddy face was expressionless. He didn't quite know what to expect. He heard of Detective McGuinness but didn't know him well.

"Did you know the tea bag was invented by an American? The yanks are always looking for labor-saving devices. In the old days, my mom would never use them, thought they were a sacrilege. I don't see the difference myself as long as the tea is fresh."

"And now we have coffee bags, Sergeant. These replaced the plastic cups, millions of which are still riding out there in the ocean. The guy who invented these—another American—is now doing penance for his major contribution to global pollution." Declan then slapped the Red Green file on the desk. "The task at hand, Sergeant, is for you to tell me why there are no records of witness statements or interviews in this file."

The ridges in Twomey's forehead puckered, and he said, "They're in another folder, Detective. The boys at Cork only gave you one folder, and I think I know why. One folder was labeled 'Red Green' and the other 'Scarlet Kelly.' Garda Brannigan here did this to preserve the privacy of the victim. We didn't want the folder with the nude photos to get around, what with Nosey Nelligans coming in here. The district must have thought it was a separate case."

"You're kidding me," said Declan.

"No, Detective. You see, red and green are the colors suggested by Scarlet Kelly's name."

Twomey seemed momentarily proud of this creative eponym.

"Call me Mac," returned Declan. "Detective McGuinness is on my nameplate back in Dublin."

Twomey failed to suggest any similar informality for himself.

"Okay, Mac. Brannigan will get you a copy of his witness notes. I'll call Mooney, the medical examiner, and let him know you'll be coming over."

It was clear that Sergeant Pat Twomey felt uncomfortable with visitors from on high. Declan thought this was just as well because he preferred this response to one of oily obsequiousness. He thought of calling Cork District to have them hunt for the second file folder, but that could wait. He had a hunch that he would have to do his own interviews after he looked at and evaluated Brannigan's notes.

As it turned out, the statements were a mixed bag. The right questions were asked of some of the people living along Scilly Walk, even though not much intelligence was gained. At least some things could be ruled out, and this could be valuable for saving time. The notes for the chap that found the body were short on detail and indicated that the interviewee was definitely antagonistic to the Gardai. Perhaps there was some antagonism going the other way too. Brannigan didn't seem to be a paragon of empathy.

Declan wondered how the fisherman came to be on the beach at the particular spot the body was found. Also, he wanted to know what light he could shed on the tides and currents in the Bandon.

The forensics medical examiner was given space in an adjacent wing of Kinsale Hospital. This afforded logistical and administrative advantages and provided adequate office and storage areas. The examiner, Doctor Mooney, was a short, chunky person with well-muscled arms and a pleasant twinkle. He greeted Declan effusively as he rolled out Scarlet Kelly's body.

"Doctor Mooney, our victim was a prior drug user, and I was wondering if you're absolutely satisfied that there was no evidence of any drug…" Declan was stopped short.

Mooney held up a stubby finger and said, "I received a call from the National Drugs and Organized Crime Bureau last week, and they asked me if I ran a test for lyminiol. As you know, that's one of the new psychotropics, not covered in the normal tox screens. That drug shows up as an ENG protein in the liver, but I don't have the equipment here to test for it."

"I've heard of it, Doc, but why were they interested in that?" asked Declan.

"Apparently, it's now the drug de jour in the southern region, and it's becoming a serious problem. Also, they knew that Scarlet Kelly was using it three years ago." Mooney circled the table and picked up a small vial. "I sent a sample of tissue to Cork, and I just got the results this morning. Guess what?" he added. "I'll have to revise my report: positive for lyminiol."

"Okay. I'm not an expert, but that drug is supposed to stay in the user's system for months. Can we tell when she last ingested it?"

"Sure," said Mooney. "Judging by the rate the protein deteriorates, the lab puts it at six weeks ago. That would be just before her death."

CHAPTER 4

The medical examiner didn't have much to add about the rope fibers found on Scarlet's ankle. They would have come from a typical nylon braided line, which could be found on thousands of boats, big and small. Or the rope could have come from any one of a thousand outlets in Europe. Maybe the fisherman could offer something constructive. He was next on Declan's interview list.

Declan decided to get some lunch at a pub in the center of town. He had a yen for seafood, a dish of chowder, and thought this might be a way to open a discussion of Kinsale fishing with some of the locals. The chowder turned out to be gourmet quality, very good indeed.

There were lots of tourists in Kinsale this time of year, and accommodations were scarce and expensive. Many of the professional fishermen stayed on their boats and chartered them for shark and other fishing. There were also more formal charter services on and around the marinas.

Declan thought it more likely that Enda McDonough, the fisherman who found Scarlet Kelly's body, was an occasional crew member for one of the charters, since he had a local address and no boat of his own. McDonough told Garda Brannigan that he worked odd jobs to take care of his mother and didn't have a mobile where he could be reached.

The pub owner knew nothing about Enda, except that he seemed to show up at funerals to trade anecdotes about the deceased and check out the ladies. On these occasions he would dress formally by adding a tie to his everyday wardrobe.

Declan decided he would check out his address and see if he could catch him home. If that didn't work, he thought he could peruse the obituaries at the newspaper office for a clue as to where he might show up socially. A second stop could be the Castlepark Marina.

Things became easier when Enda turned out to be home, a run-down cottage on an attractive street lined with overgrown trees. Enda was disheveled and sucking on a cinnamon stick. This was something occasionally done in the old days by folk trying to quit tobacco cigarettes. When Enda saw Declan's Gardai identification, he said he would prefer to talk to him outside. He didn't want any of his prized possessions stolen and was convinced that this was what the Gardai did, along with their primary job of "annoying the hell out of people."

Declan thought he would try a smoother approach by saying, "How about you and I get a brew and a sandwich and have a little talk?"

Enda's eyebrows raised, and a toothy grin came on his face.

"Now you're talking, Bucky. You can't be from the Kinsale Station. You've definitely got some style if you know what I mean. Mom's been taken to a tea and doesn't need watching right this minute, so I'm free to join you."

They went to the same place Declan had lunch earlier, and Enda ordered a Murphy and a BLT. He buried his face in the plate and practically inhaled the sandwich. Then he held the plate up in the air and licked off remnants of mayonnaise. Declan glanced around nervously, but no one seemed to take notice.

"I didn't tell that shite, Brannigan, much, you know. I said he worked in the second-best retirement home in Kinsale, and he got all pissy," Enda said.

"Of course," Declan added. "Nobody likes to be second best. Forget Brannigan for now. Tell me how you came to find the body over in Scilly."

"I walk along there often, you know, looking for stuff that washes up. I never saw a body before though." Enda had finished his Murphy and was shaking his mug. Declan ordered him another. "I could see she was a beautiful girl, even though it was getting dark, and she was bloated from being in the water. Damn shame. Of course, I didn't know her," he lied.

"Did you see any evidence of foul play, like blood, clothing, anything?"

"No, but I did see some rope marks on her right ankle," Enda said between sips.

"Amazing. You never mentioned that to Brannigan. What did you think about the rope?"

"It wasn't blue," he said. "Most of the boat line around here is blue. I know. I've worked on a lot of boats. Kinsale must have gotten a truckload of blue rope sometime back, and they're still pushing it out there."

"This means that if that rope came from a boat, it probably wasn't local?"

Declan thought that Scarlet's body was probably pushed or thrown from a boat or barge because she was dead before she hit the water, there being no water in her lungs.

Declan thanked Enda, paid the bill, and left him nursing the dregs of his Murphy ale. He would have to get back to the Gardai Station and request the services of Brannigan and Daly to check with the registry and get a list of visitor boats in port.

Declan brought Twomey and Brannigan up to speed on his investigation and made a list for Brannigan to use when he started checking out the boats. Sergeant Twomey was glad to see Brannigan's and Daly's services put to use but wasn't convinced visitor boat checks would yield results. Still, it was a lot better than checking every boat in the harbor, an insurmountable task given the man-power requirement.

Declan called Gardai Cork District to check in, pick up any mail, and bring the superintendent up to speed on the case. The superintendent asked to be notified immediately if any evidence of trafficking in lyminiol turned up. If so, he would get an assist from the drug squad.

Lyminiol was a new drug, surging in popularity because it enabled users to go a long time between hits. The long-lasting occasional jolts of endorphin with surprisingly little to no bad side effects had obvious appeal. The downside was that the drug gradually destroyed the liver, resulting in an early death. It was like smoking tobacco, which gradually eroded the lungs. Lyminiol was on the controlled substances list, and enterprises caught manufacturing or selling the drug could be exposed to stiff criminal penalties.

Drugs of all kinds were increasingly finding their way to the southern coast of Ireland, and criminals took advantage of the cover afforded by a burgeoning tourist industry. It was for this reason that the two principal things on the list he gave to Brannigan were first, any evidence of blood, and second, signs of drugs. Drug-sniffing dogs and handlers could be supplied by the district, if justified.

Declan also made a call to Caitlin to get Foley's mobile number. His old friend from OSU, Bob Foley, probably didn't know he was in town, and he didn't want to surprise him. Having a representative of the Gardai pop in out of the blue could be a little disconcerting, especially since his daughter was involved with Bob's son.

As it turned out, Bob was quite surprised when Declan called and doubly surprised when he was told that Caitlin, whom he just met, was Declan's daughter. They made an appointment to get together at the Rock the following morning and catch up on the years. Besides, Declan said, he wanted to find out if Bob knew anything about the body found on the Scilly beach a month ago. Bob said he saw pictures of the girl in the *Journal* but didn't think he could contribute much to Declan's investigation. He was in the States when the body was found.

Declan was about to head back to Cork when he received a call from Sergeant Pat Twomey.

"We checked with the registry, Mac, and there are six visitor boats in the harbor right now: four French, one Dutch, one German. Brannigan and Daly will be checking them out."

"Good, Pat. We could show them a photo of Scarlet Kelly. Contact the father in Waterford and see if he has an old photo which we can age advance with software. We can use a photo of the dead girl's face for reference. The guys at the district know how to do this."

On the way back to Cork, Declan decided to call Honey.

"Caitlin is doing fine," he told her. "I'm meeting with the father of the guy she's dating tomorrow."

"Omigod! Are things that serious already?" Honey said.

"No, no. Her boyfriend's father is an old acquaintance."

Declan realized that he may have provided too much information at this stage in the game. He would be deluged with questions for the duration of his stay in the south.

He arrived at the motel later than he hoped and struggled into an adjacent pub for a bite and a brew. When he finally reached his room, he undressed and went straight to bed.

CHAPTER 5

In the morning, Declan showered and shaved then downed a breakfast of eggs, black-and-white pudding, hash browns, bread, and coffee.

On the way to the Rock, the robo car swerved to avoid a large branch in the road and deftly avoided a vehicle coming in the opposite direction.

"I'll never get used to these things," he muttered.

The car sped into the advancing sunlight, and it started to rain. The car then automatically slowed in response to the sensory hits of a thousand water drops. The rain suddenly stopped, and the fragrance of sweet grass entered the ventilator. The car resumed its speed.

By the time he got to the Lower Road, he decided to park in a lay-by and take Scilly Walk up to the Rock. This would enable him to enjoy the morning after-the-rain sensation and also check out the beach where Scarlet Kelly's body was found.

This was not a beach of sand and smooth contours but a rough collection of mossy rocks and occasional scrubby vegetation. Detritus washed up with the tide, and it was easy to see that it would be difficult to drag a body any distance, particularly a nude body, without scraping it up extensively on a variety of obstacles. About seventy-five meters down the shore to the east and south, a large pipe with a gravity backflow gate opened onto the beach.

There was still a crime-scene marker for the location of the body, and it was unlikely that it had been moved. This beach would not be a pleasant walk for anyone, hence the reason for the paved footpath located a few meters above. One hiked on the path, not the beach.

Declan wondered about Enda McDonough, the fisherman. He said he navigated this walk looking for "treasures" that might have washed ashore. An exaggeration. Sections of the beach could not be seen from the walk. So, in the unlikely event that he staggered over the stones, he would miss a lot of stuff. He may have occasionally walked down to the water, over the stones, and scanned up and down the beach. This was how he spotted the body apparently. So was it a truly chance encounter?

Declan made his way to the impressive oak-door entrance to Bob Foley's abode. He marveled at the polished brass shamrock on the door. Declan always had ambivalent feelings about this national symbol of Ireland. It was a most humble and mundane expression of aspiration and identity; a reminder that the irony of this plant lies in the fact that it is both ubiquitous and exceptional at the same time.

The shamrock isn't one plant but many. The magic is that, whichever plant you choose, it would always count to three: one, two, three; red, yellow, blue; ready, set, go; Father, Son, Holy Spirit; Jesus, Mary, Joseph. Three was magical.

Declan was buzzed in and met his old friend from Ohio, Bob Foley, on the driveway landing. He was cheerfully ushered into the house and offered tea and some of his daughter's scones, warmed up for the occasion.

"Caitlin made these for me when I arrived, Dec, but I'm sure you know how good a cook she is." Bob said as he settled into his favorite chair, and Declan sat opposite.

"She's a great woman—like her mother," said Declan. "But tell me, Bob. I never heard from you after your wife died. I'm pleased and amazed you surfaced again to take on the project of rehabbing this old place. I'm sure if JJ were alive, he'd love it too."

"I don't know, Dec. I sometimes regret having started this project, considering how difficult and expensive it's become. Trying to deal with an architect and contractors from four thousand miles, using e-mail and FaceTime to communicate is bad enough. Throw in the Cork County Council and the whole cockamamie Irish building system, and the recipe is a disaster."

"Bitch, bitch," said Declan. "It seems to me you've done well enough with the whole project: upgraded insulation, energy-efficient heating, the new solar energy system using the latest storage technology. Also, I like the look of the interior. The whole place blends nicely into the surroundings, but it's also very modern. Lovely job."

"Let me show you one of my favorite talking points," said Bob.

He walked Declan down a short flight of stairs and into a side room with some office furniture and storage shelves. Near one wall, a square trapdoor in the floor was covered by a rug which Bob pulled back. He unlocked the door, which opened to a steep flight of stairs leading to a darkened space below.

"This goes out to Bandon River," he said proudly.

"It's true then," said Declan. "I went to primary school in Kinsale, and the rumor when I was a kid was that old Otis Sham was a smuggler who traded in pirated goods, stuff brought in from the continent mostly. Do you mind if I go down there to check it out?"

"You are my guest, Dec. But be careful. It can be a little sloppy, particularly after a rain." Bob reached over to a wall switch. "This light will help you most of the way."

The floor of the cavern was fairly new concrete; the walls were cool and moist blocks. Eventually, the floor merged into small gravel, and the walls became rougher. The crunch of the gravel reverberated in the space, and the walls glistened with moisture. Rivulets of water ran at the base of the wall on each side. There was no pooling because the slope of the floor carried the water down to an entrance pipe, about a meter in diameter. The pipe was embedded in the exterior rock wall and was completely covered by an iron backflow gate, which opened out. The gate showed signs of age and rust. Small holes at the base of the gate allowed water to escape from inside and drain onto the beach.

Declan turned and looked back up the shaft he just descended. He could see watermarks on the walls from earlier, wetter times. He shouted up to Bob Foley to tell him he was going through the gate and onto the beach. He planned to climb to the walk and return through the oak door off Scilly Walk.

Out on the beach, Declan could see the crime-scene marker in the distance. He noted that the gate was heavy but moved fairly smoothly on the hinges. He got rust and dirt on his shirt—and a smudge of grease. Interesting.

Donal Riordan's pickup truck lumbered onto the driveway just as Declan ascended the stairs from Scilly Walk. Donal started to wrestle his mower and tools from the bed of the truck and looked at Declan as if to say, *"Who the feck are you?"*

Declan introduced himself and said his visit was both social and official, and would he mind answering a few questions regarding his investigation of Scarlet Kelly's murder.

"As I told Garda Brannigan," said Donal, "I was in Galway, visiting my sister, the week they found that unfortunate girl. I can't swear the body wasn't there the last time I was here doing maintenance, but Brannigan said it couldn't have been. I never saw that girl before and didn't know who she was."

"Tell me, Mister Riordan—Donal," said Declan. "In the course of doing your work around here, did you ever lube the gate on the pipe down on the beach?"

"Oh, that feckin' thing. No, that was Old Man Sham's escape hatch. I don't think anyone has touched it in years. And it wasn't too long ago when it was underwater." Donal turned as Bob Foley joined them on the driveway.

"How about you, Bob?" said Declan. "Have you greased that gate recently?"

"If that's been greased, Dec, then it was done by the fairies or Otis Sham's ghost," Bob said.

"It wasn't Old Sham," said Donal. "The only feckin' thing he ever greased was palms."

"The only other person who might have greased those hinges is Stitch Hegarty, our contractor. I'll give him a call and ask him," Bob said. "I also want to remind him the trapdoor was unlocked when I first came in. I locked it so I wouldn't forget later. Only he and I have a key. I like to keep it locked all the time as we normally have no reason to go through the trapdoor. Stitch, however, is still sealing the walls down there, and he has a habit of leaving it open."

Declan brushed off his shirt, and he and Bob returned to the living room. There was some more conversation about the old days, and Bob decided it was time for some Jameson.

"Tell me, Bob. You normally live over here about four months of the year and in the States the rest of the time?" Declan was puzzled. "Is it possible someone might be squatting here while you're gone?"

"No, Dec. There are no signs of that. Besides, Jimmy comes down from Cork on occasion, and Donal shows up, unannounced, to do yard work. There's also the contractor. He's not here as often as I'd like, but he comes at irregular intervals."

Bob held the Waterford carafe up to the light, studied it, then poured two more drinks for himself and Declan.

"Your security has broken down, Bob," said Declan. "Someone has gotten in here. Maybe I should say, *is* getting in here."

Between sips of whiskey, Declan's mobile signaled. It was Brannigan with news about his port activities.

"I've been aboard two of the French boats and came up dry. I have to say, the photo of the dead girl was a success. One of the frogs said he didn't know her but was sorry he didn't."

"All right, Brannigan. Two down and four to go. Tell you what. I'll go with you to the German boat. That's the big yacht, and we can take a drone out to it. Put your report and a copy of the new photo in the Red Green folder, and I'll pick it up tomorrow."

Declan thought Brannigan would appreciate the deference paid to his file naming. He also thought a little extra security might be a good thing, considering what seemed to be happening up at Bob Foley's place. Any Nosey Nelligans in the Gardai Station might spot the file but wouldn't know it contained anything of interest.

CHAPTER 6

The prow of the big yacht, *Fancy Fran*, sliced the calm blue-green water of the Adriatic Sea, pushing a bone of curling foam in its maw. The gleaming white hull with black-and-gold lettering was doing ten knots against a fair wind. In the wheelhouse, Con Mercer scanned the horizon through dark sunglasses and rubbed his sunburned nose. He turned to his skipper, Syl Thornberg, and asked how long it would take to reach Kinsale Harbour.

Captain Thornberg gave his boss his best estimate, considering all the nautical signposts and weather forecasts available to him from the considerable technology of the vessel. Two stops were planned en route to charge cells, replenish supplies, and check on some of Mercer's real estate. Some more party time wasn't out of the question.

"I'd say we had a good stay off Trieste, Mr. Mercer," the captain said. "The refugee vessel from Croatia turned out to be a useful diversion. The EDF coast guard was distracted long enough to allow us to load the merchandise without incident."

"They wouldn't bother us, Syl. We're just some rich guys with a yacht, entertaining bigwigs with wine, caviar, and a bevy of party girls." But Mercer thought to himself that his wife, Frances, parading on board with tens of thousands of euros worth of newly purchased jewelry, might attract the attention of Customs.

Mercer's fixer, Doug "Meatface" Henson hired half a dozen Italian hostesses to cater to the guests but let them go before they pulled anchor. They were very friendly to Doug when they left the motor launch, smothering his scarred-up face with kisses.

Scarlet Kelly, the beautiful Irish hostess, was on board the entire trip and would remain as a "guest" until they returned to Kinsale. She was Mercer's special preserve, much to the chagrin of Frances Mercer.

Conrad and Frances Mercer had been married for six years. She was at least fifteen years his junior and knew full well that her good looks and social skills were bedrock for the marriage. They had no children and didn't plan to. Mercer had no desire to share his good fortunes with any progeny, and this suited Frances fine.

Still, Frances had to contend with a long line of beautiful women who circled Con like sharks, waiting for an opening. She always held her own but wasn't getting any younger. She planned on enjoying and enhancing her lifestyle for a long time and built her own bank account as a hedge against any downturn. Her husband didn't know about this and thought that Frances limited herself to stockpiling jewelry, expensive clothing, and gay friends.

Scarlet Kelly was a stunning girl and a special threat. Con seemed to like everything about her, even though she was a bit of a junkie. (Hell, who wasn't junked up on something these days?)

Scarlet had a knack for getting what she wanted from anyone who crossed her path. "That bitch could spread for any man or woman with the right calling card," Frances once told Doug. Con thought of her as an asset in more ways than one, and it scared the hell out of Frances.

Con went forward to spend time with Scarlet, who was sunbathing in a bikini and reading a paperback.

"Would you like a frozen martini, sweetheart?" he purred. "A lot of the staff was let go, but we still have a bartender."

"Sure, Mr. Mercer," she said. "If you'll join me, I will." She undid her bra, rolled over, and smiled. "Could you rub a little lotion on my back?"

Con reached over to the intercom on the bulkhead, ordered the drinks, then rubbed lotion on his hands before applying it to the smooth, expectant skin on Scarlet Kelly's back. The bartender soon arrived with the drinks on a small silver plate. He handed out two white cloth serviettes, embellished with the logo "F F."

Con handed Scarlet a tiny packet of lyminiol and said, "This will add a little extra zest to your drink, Scarlet, give you an appetite for all sorts of things." He ran his hand over Scarlet's thigh, and she didn't object.

"I think I've had enough sun for the day, Mr. Mercer. You know we Irish are fair-skinned and not used to it." Scarlet was starting to slur her words ever so slightly. "I think I'll take a nap. Maybe you would care to join me?"

At that moment Con felt urges he hadn't experienced in a while, even given his matrimonial affinity for Fran's attractive loins. There was no hesitation in his acceptance of Scarlet's invitation.

Con Mercer spoke three languages, an ability put to frequent use in his forays around the continent. His yacht, which he obviously christened for his wife in a brighter moment, was built and registered in Germany. He normally transacted business in English, as did most of the global community; but for special moments, he frequently effused in French or German.

Fran lingered in the shadows, some distance from Scarlet's stateroom. She saw Con and Scarlet enter and raged silently, biting her lip. There would have to be a come-to-Jesus meeting with that son of a bitch very soon. She thought about bursting into Scarlet's room but didn't want to give the impression that she really gave a damn. She did, but for now she would contain her anger and wait for the right moment.

The night passed slowly as the *Fancy Fran* coursed through the Mediterranean, heading for an anchorage off Capitano on the island of Sardinia. The moon glittered brightly from the small waves, meeting the foaming crests along the coast. Con Mercer wanted to check out some property here currently half submerged.

Fran and Con were sharing some wine in their large stateroom, and Fran now decided to confront her husband.

"Darling," she said with sarcasm. "I've been suffering your peccadilloes with the opposite sex for a few years now, but this time your extracurricular relationship has gone too far. Scarlet Kelly is a jumped-up bimbo who seems to have wheedled her way into your brain like a cancer. An affair with this whore will destroy our marriage."

"Darling," said Con with equal sarcasm. "This is not a relationship or an affair. Scarlet is simply an appetizer before the main course, and you are still the main course. You would be able to see that if you stepped away from your baubles and silly friends long enough."

"Bullshit. That girl is the appetizer, main course, and dessert. Since we left Kinsale, you've spent most of your time with her when we're not doing a formal meet and greet or hosting parties."

Fran was visibly flushed and upset. With feigned obsequiousness, Con encircled Fran's waist and pulled her close.

"This is nonsense, Fran. Scarlet is simply a piece of candy. When we get back to Kinsale, she'll be on her way, just like all the other hostesses we bring on board—temporary help."

Con tried to go further but found he was played out.

It was a clear, sunny morning, and Doug Henson was throwing scraps of food to gulls circling the small boat ramp on the stern of the yacht. He was waiting for Con to join him for a trip to Con's beach property on Capitano. Doug was wearing sunglasses and had rubbed sun lotion all over his sensitive, scarred face. He smiled at the greedy grabs of the birds, but it was difficult to tell when Doug was smiling. His mouth contorted into a half grimace.

Doug Henson was raised by a Chinese-American couple who traveled on business between Hong Kong and the States. He was with the couple when they were killed in a fiery plane crash. Doug was eighteen at the time and was severely burned in the accident. His current face is the result of several operations, and he was told he was lucky to be alive. Since then, however, Doug's scrapes put him in even-greater jeopardy and improved his survivorship skills. As "Meatface" in the drug trade, he became a feared adversary, who usually came out on the winning side of any tangle. Con Mercer hired Doug for his proven "problem-solving" talents.

Con greeted Doug and told him to crank up the boat. They rode the boat down the ramp and headed for Capitano coast.

"I've received reports, Doug, that the Capitano 620 beach plot now has twice as much sand above water at high tide."

"That's great, Boss," Henson said. "We could probably build on some of it now if we could get approval from the Italians. In the meantime, we have a great, deserted beach to run our product in."

"Yeah, and the EDF will see us as coastal developers, not drug runners," said Con. It's a win-win for Mercer Enterprises. "Let's check the water levels over there and see how it matches up with last time. I want to have something good to report to the Coastal Development Commission."

CHAPTER 7

D eclan was tucking into a plate of pancakes and sausage when Brannigan signaled on his mobile.

"Nothing of interest to report on the boat interviews. The captain on the Dutch boat was very nervous the whole time we were on his boat. He had a big dog on board that kept growling at us, and he finally said we would need a warrant to look at anything."

"Did you tell him you would come back with the Coast Guard, who wouldn't need any special warrant?" Declan wasn't sure about this, but it sounded good.

"I told him we could come back with a drug-sniffing dog, and it wouldn't be healthy for his dog. He finally agreed to let us look around. We found no indications of blood or drugs, and he said they never saw anyone that looked like Scarlet Kelly," said Brannigan.

Garda Brannigan came from a long line of police. With the exception of a few vocations to the priesthood or convent, all the Brannigan clan showed fealty to the badge and the virtues of law and order; regulations strictly applied. He was glad to be working with Inspector McGuinness as he thought Sergeant Twomey had become too comfortable and laid-back for proper police work.

Brannigan decided one day to spark up the image of the Kinsale Station by pinning up a collection of insignia from law-enforcement organizations all over the world. These were collected in trades with tourists who were usually cops on vacation. The exchanges frequently occurred in pubs along with stories of colorful and dangerous police activities of a kind Brannigan could only dream about. Sergeant Twomey was amused by the display but didn't object.

Declan wanted Brannigan to accompany him out to the German yacht, *Fancy Fran*, but said he would need another day to check out some things in Cork. The district told him that information from Scarlet Kelly's drug arrest three years earlier showed that at the time Kelly was working as a hostess in a nightclub called the Paradise Club. Kelly had been arrested in a raid on a high-priced brothel, which had no apparent connection with the Paradise.

"I know that nightclub," Brannigan said. "But not in any official capacity. I was there for a District promotion party about five years ago. I have a hazy memory of bawdy singing and gals in slinky dresses. If you're going there, Inspector, you better watch your back."

"More likely my wallet."

Declan and Brannigan laughed and ended the conversation.

After calling his daughter to make some small talk and cancel out on dinner, Declan called the Paradise to set up a meeting. The club was closed, but the proprietor, Stella Murphy, would be available in her office until 1630 hours. She didn't sound too pleased about meeting with a representative of the Gardai and sighed with raspy resignation.

The Paradise Club was a low, modern structure located off Western near Woods. The office was located to the rear, and the door was unlocked. Stella Murphy was seated behind a large desk, fronted by a sign which read, "*The buck stops here—to take a piss.*" She was an older woman with a face wrinkled by years of smoking cigarettes and squinting into gloomy surroundings.

She studied Declan's identification cautiously, tapped an ash from a cigarette, and said, "What can I do for you, Inspector McGuinness?"

Declan showed Stella the photo, which Brannigan left for him at the Station, and said, "This is Scarlet Kelly. She worked for you three years ago and had some trouble with drugs. What can you tell me about her?"

Stella said she didn't know anything about drugs. Kelly was sent over by Kilbarry Agency, a company which specialized in providing temporary help of all kinds. It was to be a few nights doing hostess work for the college crowd. She didn't know Scarlet at all and relied on the agency to vet the girls. She gave Declan the address of the agency and reiterated that there was no drug-dealing going on in her place.

The Kilbarry Agency was an old brick building on Sullivan Quay. It was late in the afternoon when Declan arrived, but the owner of the company promised he would hang around to answer any questions Declan might have.

A breeze was gusting along the quay, coming all the way from the ocean to the south. A tinge of wetness was in the air, not unusual for most locations year-round in this part of Ireland.

The front door of the agency opened into a large, musty room filled with old wood and metal cabinets. A small man with thick glasses greeted Declan and led him to a back office.

"We don't have much in the way of computers, Inspector, so it may take me a while to find what you're looking for."

Declan was amazed that any employment agency could operate without computers, relying on filing cabinets and paper folders to conduct business. He soon learned that the agency was set up to operate on a clever combination of automated and manually filed data. The owner, Cornelius Kilbarry, would enter the name of a client in his office computer, which would search and return a code number. This number would direct him to a matching numbered file in the outer room. The file would contain personal information on the client and another code reference. The second code reference could then be entered in the computer, and employment and other information would be displayed without any mention of the client's name.

"If my computer is ever hacked, my client list and their personal information is protected," Kilbarry said. "It may seem cumbersome to you, but I can't afford IT services and encryption technology."

"Yeah," said Declan. "What happens when you run out of warehouse space for hard-copy files? Building rental on the quay must be expensive."

"I plan to retire and sell the business in two years, and I won't run out of space in that time. Also, this building needs to be brought up to code. If I want to remain here and avoid a big insurance increase, I'll have to put in sprinklers," said Kilbarry.

Kilbarry also said he vetted client information like licenses, school and police records, employment background, and personal and professional recommendations. Declan doubted how good these checks were. Mention of Kelly's drug arrest was absent from her file, and there was a paucity of any other relevant information.

Ultimately, Declan got what he came for. Two months before her death, Scarlet Kelly was referred to Doug Henson, Mercer Enterprises representative, for hostess duties on the company yacht moored in Kinsale Harbour. A mobile number was included.

Declan returned to his motel to put what he learned in perspective. It appeared that person or persons unknown on the *Fancy Fran* were likely the last ones to see Scarlet Kelly alive.

Declan woke to a rainy morning. Even though the motel was well-insulated and seemed to soak up most of the noise, there was a downspout outside one of the windows that emitted a load and persistent *drip, drip, drip*. Three again. He counted the rhythmic one, two, three over and over in his head. It finally stopped, and he caught a glimpse of sunlight on the dresser.

He showered and dressed but was preoccupied with thoughts of the yacht and how best to handle the interview and search. He could get a warrant, but that would take some time, and he might scare off the culprit. If one of the crew was the killer, he or she could jump ship and disappear in the countryside. Also, if the yacht pulled anchor and slipped miles out to sea, he would have to convince Interpol and the EDF coast guard to chase them down. That could get tricky because he only had suspicions and no real evidence. For all he knew, Scarlet could have gotten in a fight with a prostitute who then took her out and dumped her in the Bandon—unlikely, but possible.

Best he could tell, Scarlett was not a prostitute. But she was very attractive and would have been resented by the typical street girls. Declan thought it much more likely that she was connected in some way with one of the higher-ups, perhaps a Mercer executive. As some of the Kinsale fisherfolk would say: she would have been a keeper.

Declan thought he might have another problem. He knew nothing about yachts. Though he was raised in Kinsale and Dublin and spent a year in the United States, taking courses at Ohio State University, he had never been on a boat longer than ten meters.

He wished he had his friend, Bob Foley, with him. As a retired naval officer, Bob could be his technical advisor. He might have to make some notes and ask Bob questions later. It could be an excuse to see the Rock again and relieve Bob of some of his Jameson. Bob didn't have a lot of sea duty in his career and, as he remembered from Bob's tales, never commanded a vessel. Still, he would have a lot more nautical knowledge at his disposal than Declan could ever muster.

CHAPTER 8

Declan arrived at Kinsale Station in time to see Brannigan adding another patch to his wall collection. This was a US Drug Enforcement Agency jacket breast patch acquired from a burly special agent on vacation. The agent was extolling the magnificence of his Celtic heritage and was well lubricated with Smithwick's red ale when he made the emblem trade.

"Before we hit the yacht, Brannigan, we need to have a plan of action. Finish with your decorating, and give me an ear," Declan said.

Brannigan sat next to Declan and opened his notebook.

"We didn't get through the last French boat, Inspector, but from what you're telling me, it looks like the big yacht is where Scarlet Kelly spent her last days."

"That's right. And we might find some indication that's where she was killed. We'll need to question everyone on the boat," said Declan.

"It's likely some or even most of the crew may not be available to interrogate. I'll get a complete list from this guy, Doug Henson, and see if any of them have a record," said Brannigan.

"Some of the hostesses that were sent there with Kelly are probably still onboard, working every day. The Mercers are having parties for the locals and politicians in conjunction with the Annual Gourmet Festival. Let's go over low-key," said Declan. "Your friendly Gardai, seeing how we can be of assistance."

Declan then called Doug Henson at the number provided by Kilbarry and confirmed the appointment.

Sergeant Pat Twomey stepped in from his office to say that the drone was waiting for them up on the pad in Cappagh. Everyone referred to any automatically piloted aerial vehicle as a drone, whether it was a small surveillance craft or a five-passenger quad copter. He asked Declan if he would have any problem programming the robot, and Declan said he wouldn't.

The drone was a large bright-yellow machine capable of carrying four persons. There was a Lundqvist 670 electric motor at the end of each of four arms, radiating from the center cab. Propellers at the top of each motor turned slowly in the morning breeze. The motors were powered by a high-capacity central storage cell, which received its charge from a solar and biofuel-powered induction plate on top of the pad. A gray-and-blue Gardai logo was inscribed on each of the four arms.

"Well, Brannigan," said Declan, "this is hardly going in low-key, but at least I won't get seasick on the launch."

Declan climbed onto a padded seat, hooked his belt, leaned over, and brought up a map of the Bandon River and Kinsale Harbor on a large console screen. He moved a cursor to an image of the yacht, typed in a Gardai code, and pressed the *Go* button after checking with Brannigan. A mechanical, "Stand clear," sounded three times, and the engines whirred to life and lifted the drone into the blue morning sky.

Con Mercer and Doug Henson were standing on the yacht helideck to greet Declan and Brannigan. Following introductions, the drone engines wound down, and sounds of music could be heard coming from speakers in the sundeck saloon. Declan could see several young women dressed in black-and-silver uniforms, circulating among tables with seated guests.

Declan took note of Henson's extensively scarred face but avoided staring or looking away. This was the normal reaction of someone wishing to convey an "appearances don't upset me" pose. Conversely, disfigured individuals frequently regarded such a pose as politely patronizing. Their counter position might be "beg me to tell you how I got this way, but I won't." But there was something else unusual about Doug Henson, and Declan tried to put his finger on it. He felt he had known Henson somewhere else.

"Please come into the lounge, Inspector. It's more private and less noisy. I can offer you something to eat or drink while we talk." Con was at his unctuous best.

"No, thank you, Mr. Mercer. Perhaps later," said Declan. "As I told Mr. Henson, we're investigating the death of Scarlet Kelly, who was in your employ as a temporary hostess six weeks ago."

"Yes, Inspector, she would have left us about that time for another job. She was a lovely girl, very much alive when Doug—Mr. Henson—dropped her ashore in Kinsale. I am very sad to hear about her death. How did this happen?" Con glanced at Doug, who was expressionless. "I've been occupied with business meetings and legal matters and haven't been paying attention to the news," Con added.

"I didn't know either, Inspector, or I would have told Mr. Mercer. I took her over to Kinsale in the small boat at the end of her gig," said Doug Henson, pointing to the ramp at the stern of the yacht.

"The girl's body was found on Scilly beach. She had been stabbed to death," said Declan. "I'd like Garda Brannigan to look at that small boat with you, Mr. Henson."

Con was visibly upset, and Declan thought his reaction was genuine. But there was also an element of concern in his manner.

Doug and Brannigan left, and Con Mercer made arrangements for each of the crew to come to the lounge to talk privately to Declan. The photo was only needed for two of the crew, as all the others knew Scarlet. Some had heard the news that her body had been found, but no one wanted to get involved with the police. The cook, Bertha Maloney, mentioned that Con Mercer was quite taken with Scarlet and probably had a closer relationship than his wife would have preferred.

When questioned about his relationship with Scarlett, Con Mercer said he considered her like a daughter.

"My wife, Fran liked her too," he lied.

Declan asked if he could speak to his wife, and Con said Frances left yesterday for Madrid to spend some time with a sick friend. He himself would join her in two days, but they would be coming straight back after that.

Con took Declan up to the bridge to meet Captain Syl Thornberg, who was scratching notes on a chart, while his first officer looked on.

"How long will the yacht be in Kinsale?" asked Declan. "The registry said you plan to weigh anchor in another twenty days."

"That's Mr. Mercer's plan," said Thornberg. "We have some stops in France to meet with coastal authorities and others as long as the weather doesn't give us problems. We'll provide you with a schedule, Inspector."

At the end of the day, Brannigan and Henson met with Declan and Mercer in the bar above the galley. Most of the crew, guests, and hostesses had gone ashore in the launch, and a second round of guests was scheduled to come onboard that evening. Declan wanted to be finished and gone by that time. He and Brannigan had the definite impression that the welcome mat might be wearing thin.

Declan asked Brannigan how his visit to the small boat went.

"Everything is 'Red Green' on that boat," said Brannigan.

Con Mercer looked puzzled. He raised his wineglass halfway before he set it back down on the shiny black counter.

"That's police code, Mr. Mercer," Declan lied. "It means we will have to take the small boat for a full forensics workup. I hope you can do without it until we have this case settled."

Declan knew that Brannigan was telling him there was a strong reason to believe the boat was used to transport the body.

"I can get another boat temporarily, Inspector, but I definitely want a receipt for this one," said Henson.

Con Mercer reddened with anger as he said, "I haven't insisted on a warrant, Inspector McGuinness, and I won't now. Take the damn boat, but you won't find a thing."

"Garda Brannigan said the boat smelled like bleach," Doug said. "I told him that we used that boat for shark-fishing last week. We didn't catch anything, but the chum used for bait had sloshed all over the bottom. We used the bleach to kill the smell."

"We'll check it out. Hope you did a thorough job," Declan said, glaring at Henson.

Earlier Mercer had taken Declan on a quick tour of the yacht. Declan noted that everything was spic and span, perfect, including Scarlet's stateroom. Actually, Scarlet had stayed in two staterooms: the first with one of the other girls, and the second when Con had set her up with a private room. There was no clothing or personal items in either stateroom. Con said she took all that stuff with her when she left with Doug.

Declan thought that if Scarlet was killed on the yacht, the galley would have been a likely place. A kitchen knife was used, and the cook, Bertha, said one of her set was missing. The galley smelled faintly of bleach, but that wouldn't be unusual.

CHAPTER 9

Declan sent Brannigan back with the small boat, which was delivered to a Gardai impound area near Ringrone on the Bandon River. Declan flew back to Cappagh in the drone. He could have sent the drone back on its own and rode with Brannigan, but he wanted to avoid the choppy waters that accompanied the afternoon weather change. To Declan, sailing the waters of any Atlantic Ocean tributary was an invitation to violent digestive disruption. He was certainly an anomaly for anyone raised in Kinsale, but this didn't embarrass him.

Back at the Gardai Station, Brannigan was printing photos of the *Fancy Fran* employees, which he took with his mobile. He was also entering the names provided by Doug Henson into the classified Gardai Records Search Program. All US and European data bases would be cross-checked.

Sergeant Twomey came out of his office, swinging a dried tea bag held between two fingers.

"Would anyone like some tea?"

"How many times do you plan to use that tea bag, Sergeant?" asked Declan. "I thought you were the man that insisted on fresh tea."

"Oh no, Inspector Mac," said Twomey, pointing to a jar containing dried teabags. "These I save for my orchids, to add to the bark, you know."

Declan thought to himself that only in the Kinsale Gardai Station would you find an orchid collection in the sergeant's office. He carelessly picked up one of the dried tea bags and swung it gently by the small string. He suddenly brightened.

"Wait a minute. Brannigan, bring up the photos you took of the small boat."

"There you are," said Declan. "Look at that one—good photos, by the way. The anchor leaning against the boat box looks brand new, and it's tied to a coil of blue rope! That anchor and line were bought in Kinsale."

"So maybe the old one got broken," said Twomey, who took the answer to his tea question to be yes.

"No. Anchors aren't easily broken. They last forever. I suspect the original is at the bottom of Bandon River, having been used to weigh down Scarlet Kelly."

Declan stirred a sugar into the tea offered by Sergeant Twomey.

Brannigan, who had no small experience with boats, studied the photos again and said, "That knot tied to the anchor doesn't look right. The over and under is wrong. It's a granny knot, not a reef knot or something stronger, maybe tied in a hurry. That wouldn't hold."

"That's it, Brannigan," said Declan. "If he tied the old rope to Scarlet's leg in a similar manner, it would explain why she came loose and floated. He never expected that body to surface again. Must have been a heart-stopper for him when the body was found washed up."

"God, I hope we can find some DNA from Scarlet Kelly on that boat. Doug Henson wouldn't be able to explain that so easily, and we'd have his ass nailed," said Brannigan.

"Henson dumped the body. He either killed Scarlet, or he knows who did. I'd bet my pension on it," said Declan. "I can't wait to see what comes up on the records search. Also, we need to find some motive."

"You all did good," said Twomey. "Now it's time for a little pub food."

He carefully watered his orchids with a little can.

Declan left Brannigan with instructions to check area nautical suppliers for information on any recent purchase of line and anchor. Brannigan said he knew the best place to start with that.

"Show them the photos you took of the people we interviewed on the yacht in case Henson sent someone else."

Declan thought he might pay Bob Foley a visit before he returned to his motel in Cork. Perhaps they could go out for grub at the Dungeon, a new place in Scilly he heard about. The fare was supposed to be excellent, and the Annual Gourmet Festival was in full swing. First, though, he had to call the Cork District and give the superintendent an update on the case.

The district superintendent, Sean McCarthy, was a man in his fifties with considerable survival skills and many scars from years of political infighting in the bureaucracy. He was well-liked in the Gardai as a man who would have your back in a tight scrape.

"I'm taking heat from Dublin, Mac. Too many college kids are getting laced with lyminiol, and now the latest thing—mixing it with cocaine for a super high. Two dealers arrested up north said they're getting their stuff from towns in the southern region. A trafficker arrested in Waterford was killed last week before he could testify. The drug squad has no leads."

"Well, there are some shady characters on the *Fancy Fran*, Chief," said Declan. "I'll know more when I get record results in the morning. The computer down here has been very slow today. So far, we found no obvious signs of drugs, but Mercer Enterprises would be an ideal cover, and Doug Henson is definitely a person of interest."

"I'm going to set up a raid on the yacht by the drug squad. Given the developments with the Scarlet Kelly case, and the fact that she was a user, I think I can sell it. Con Mercer can fulminate all he wants when he gets back from Madrid."

Superintendent McCarthy wished Declan well and ended the call.

Declan walked out into the evening air. A bright moon was crossing a blanket of soft gray cumulus, unfurling like a comforter on a great bed. It would probably be raining within the hour, but Declan hoped to be sipping Jameson with Bob Foley in the Rock by that time.

Two small drones were crossing in the sky above, carrying packages that looked like groceries. Declan remembered when small drones came into widespread use in Ireland. He thought they would become easy targets for pranksters with long rifles, but none of that ever happened. Firearms were not ubiquitous, like in the States, and were eventually replaced by highly concentrated lasers (HCLs). Now HCLs are even more regulated than conventional firearms, and only the military and law enforcement have access to them. Still—mischievously—Declan pointed his finger, with thumb up, and pretended he was popping off the drones.

There would be hell to pay in Kinsale if the *Fancy Fran* were raided. How does one keep a drug raid low-key? The superintendent would probably have to involve the coast guard to ferry the Gardai to the yacht. He thought that if Mercer and crew got wind of the raid, they would weigh anchor and leave for sure. If the CG tried to stop them, there could be fireworks. He didn't think Captain Syl Thornberg would want to endanger anyone, but he might not be giving the orders.

Bob Foley had drink in hand when he greeted Declan at the door, "Welcome back to the Rock."

Bob had a head start and was unusually mellow.

"Let me show you a picture, Bob, and get your professional naval opinion."

Declan had Brannigan send copies of all his yacht pics to his mobile and proceeded to tell Bob about his meeting with Mercer and Henson.

"This guy, Henson, says he was shark-fishing in this boat," Declan said, handing his mobile to Bob.

"I doubt he was deep-sea fishing in this, Dec," said Bob. "This boat isn't rigged out for large poles, and there's no evidence of fishing gear of any kind. This is a luxury craft that matches the yacht. Look at the upholstery and fancy work."

"Those were also my thoughts. Henson is lying. I just don't know if Mercer is involved, but I don't see how he wouldn't be."

Declan drained his glass and told Bob he wanted to buy him dinner at the Dungeon.

Bob agreed but said it would be pretty late by the time they finished. He asked Declan to stay in his extra bedroom and get an earlier start. Declan declined but said he was thinking about asking Bob if he could move in and give him part of his per-diem allowance.

"That would be great, Dec," said Bob. "It would be just like when we shared a room at OSU a thousand years ago. I don't need your per diem though. Just kick in for the Jameson."

"Deal," said Declan.

CHAPTER 10

The Dungeon lived up to its name. Dim lights and low, throbbing dinner music added atmosphere to a scene of theatrical, gastronomical mummery. Manacles and chains hung from the walls, and an iron maiden stood in one corner of the large dining area. A cage hung in the center of the room over a salad bar in the shape of a torture rack. Waitresses in red satin outfits circulated with drinks and trays of food purveying wonderful smells. The perimeter of the room was hung with scenes and explanations of medieval rites. Opposite the entrance, a large picture window looked out on a moonlit Bandon River, a lowering sky, and intermittent rain.

"My god," said Declan, "the food must be outstanding here because the ambience is absolutely spooky. Who would bring their significant other to a place like this?"

"Actually, it's quite popular with the locals," said Bob. "Some of the items in the Kinsale museum are as diabolically 'delightful' as these. We're not that far removed from the Anglo and Celtic adversaries that roamed this place thousands of years ago."

The menu contained an extensive range of high-priced goodies. Declan ordered a classic shepherd's pie and a tossed salad; Bob, bacon-wrapped filet mignon and green beans almondine. They were finishing their meal with a coffee when two couples entered from the other side of the room.

"I can't believe it. That's Doug Henson and Enda McDonough with two bimbos," said Declan. "Henson is the guy I talked to on the yacht today, and the other guy, McDonough, is the one who found Kelly's body on the beach near your place."

"They spotted us, Dec," said Bob. "The one with the scarred face—Henson—is staring at me very strangely. If he wasn't with a woman, I'd say he was trying to pick me up. He gives me the creeps."

"That's the Gardai guy, McGuinness," Henson said softly to Enda, who didn't acknowledge that he had talked to Declan earlier that week. "And who is that guy with him? Do you know him?"

"That's Foley, the yank who's fixing up the house in Scilly near my winter storage spot," said Enda, almost whispering.

The two women with Doug and Enda finished their meal and left to powder their shiny noses. Doug leaned over to Enda who was still licking barbecue sauce off his fingers.

"Do you see that cage in the middle of the room, shithead? That cage was too small for most guys, so they had to scrunch up with their legs hanging over the side. They would be left hanging like that til they died of starvation. I don't have the patience for anything like that, so if I do you, it will be painful—but quick."

Enda's eyes widened as he said, "What are you talking about, Doug?"

"I know you yapped about our operations to Kelly," said Doug. "If you ever do that with someone outside our circle again, they'll find you on the beach—in pieces."

"Scarlet was harmless, Doug. She was one of my best customers. Are you saying you…"

"Let's say she met with an unfortunate accident, which she could have avoided if she hadn't yapped to you and threatened to repeat to the Gardai."

Doug squeezed the handle of his table knife and then turned to continue staring at Bob Foley across the room.

"How safe is that storage place in Scilly?" Doug changed the subject but continued squeezing his knife.

Enda was visibly uncomfortable.

"It's near Foley's house," said Enda, "but he's gone all winter, so it's mostly private. In fact, the large pipe I use runs to a passage which leads to his house. There's a contractor who works there, but he mostly stays away if he knows Foley won't be home."

Doug Henson was interested.

"What are you using now, with all the tourists around?"

"My summer stash is kept in an old crypt in a cemetery outside of town," said Enda. "No one would ever go inside there, and even if they did, the stuff is in waterproof containers hidden in the walls. It's too wet in there to use it in the winter, but for summer, it's okay."

"You're gonna get caught moving the goods back and forth, asshole. I don't like it," said Doug. "Find a way of waterproofing that crypt and keep the stuff there year-round. We're using sealed coffee pods, wrapped in shrunk plastic. Good disguise. Should stay clean and dry."

Declan returned to his motel in Cork, thinking that the coincidence of seeing Doug Henson in a restaurant was not one he would want to repeat. Both he and Bob had strange feelings of déjà vu about Henson, but nothing either one could put a finger on. Still, the meal at the dungeon was excellent, and he would eat there again; though he wouldn't bring Caitlin or Honey. He hoped that Henson would be put away soon and remove the possibility of another chance encounter.

Declan packed his bag, thinking that the opportunity to renew his friendship with Bob would be especially fruitful, considering Caitlin and Jim's situation.

Con Mercer was meeting his wife, Frances, at a luxury hotel in Madrid. Fran said she needed time away, and he respected the boundaries, which she seemed to be drawing. He would not insist on staying with her but felt that his charm—and money—would eventually win the day.

"How are you feeling, darlin?," he asked. "I was worried that you might need a doctor to look at that bruise on your head."

"Were you afraid I might forget what happened on the yacht, or perhaps hoping that I would?" she said.

After joining in the lobby, they moved to the bar, and Con ordered wine.

Fran described how she confronted Scarlet in the galley the night after they arrived in Kinsale.

"That bitch was high as a kite and wearing nothing but a bathrobe. She said she was making a snack to bring to you."

"I wasn't in her stateroom, Fran," he lied. "I was on deck, talking to Doug. He was going to ferry Scarlet over to the marina. She was supposed to be getting ready. He went down to check on her and found you two going at it, hot and heavy, in the galley."

"She said you gave her a going-away present and then took a piece of jewelry from the pocket of her robe. It was a gold brooch with diamonds and emeralds in a shamrock design, just like the one you gave me on our engagement. If you gave her that, I'd kill you, and you know it," Fran said.

"It was only your cubic zirconium copy, Fran," he said, "Sham rocks, not the real thing. Doug said you slapped Scarlet and then she hit you?"

"That whore clocked me good, hit my head when I fell and went unconscious. She was gone when Doug brought me around," she said.

"You don't remember anything?" Con asked nervously.

"Well, Doug handed the brooch to me and led me up the passage to our stateroom. My cut was sore but not bleeding much, which surprised me. There was a mess of blood in the galley," she said. "Doug said not to worry. He would take care of it."

"I apologize, Fran, for not getting to you sooner that night. I brought you an ice pack for your head, but you were sound asleep when I got to the stateroom. That worried me too because it could have been a sign of serious concussion or something," said Con.

"The only concussion in my mind was the one I needed to give you for hiring Scarlet Kelly in the first place," said Fran. "Doug told me she had drowned, and that's when I decided I needed a change of climate. Madrid sounded good, nice, and warm, away from her and away from you."

"That's all right, Darling," Con said. "I told everyone you were visiting a sick friend. The Gardai will want to talk to you when you return. You don't need to tell them about the fight with Scarlet. Doug will back you up. Tell them you lied about the sick friend. So what?"

Fran was not ready to forgive Con for being, in her view, a shit heel. However, neither she nor Con were ready to throw the relationship overboard; though it would never be quite the same after

Scarlet. She was glad Scarlet was removed permanently as a problem but didn't want to know any details about her demise.

Fran thought that Scarlet might steal the brooch copy to support her drug habit, but if she did, she wouldn't flaunt it. Yet drugs make you do funny things. Also, Con may have figured he would replace the copy later. She didn't want to think of Con being that stupid, so she'd stick with Scarlet being a thief.

CHAPTER 11

Word came to Declan early in the morning that the forensics team from Cork District found nothing of interest on the *Fancy Fran* small boat. They went over it completely and couldn't find a scrap of DNA blood evidence. But that wasn't the only piece of bad news Superintendent McCarthy shared over his mobile.

"The drug-squad raid on the yacht was not approved by the commissioner, Declan. He said Mercer has too much influence with the politicians, and the heat would be intolerable. He suggested we send in an undercover agent and try to get more positive proof before executing a raid."

McCarthy was unhappy but still convinced the *Fancy Fran* needed to be checked.

"An undercover agent is very risky, Chief," said Declan. "We could lose the initiative as well as the agent."

"I'm aware of the risk," McCarthy said. "That's why I'd like to use Garda Flaherty from Belfast. She's got the right age and looks to be a hostess, and she's done three years in Special Forces with the EDF. She comes highly recommended by the new Belfast northern district."

Shortly following the Brexit move, Northern Ireland was seriously leaning toward a referendum to join the Republic of Ireland so they could remain in the European Union. It wasn't long after that the Royal Constabulary and the Irish Gardai joined forces and reorganized themselves into the northern district of Belfast. The difficulties and problems associated with that merger were just sorting out when the Republic of Europe started to emerge from the ashes of Brexit and the EU.

Garda Brenda Flaherty was asked but was also glad to volunteer when she was told that Mercer was involved. The chance to pin something on Conrad Mercer was too good to pass up.

Mercer Enterprises was involved in the provisioning of her EDF unit with HCL arms components in Africa. The faulty housing on a shipment of energy capsules for small arms resulted in an explosion, which incinerated four Special Forces soldiers. The Mercer people blamed a Libyan supplier who was subsequently found with his throat slit. The killer was never found, but Doug Henson was in Libya at the time. Mercer Enterprises claimed no responsibility for the faulty capsules and managed to avoid prosecution because no one could come up with any evidence of wrongdoing.

"How do you want to play this?" Declan asked.

"I want you to meet Flaherty in Cork and bring her up to speed on the case," said McCarthy. "We can use Kilbarry as the referral agency and set up a bogus file and backstory. I'll cover this from my end."

"That'll work," said Declan. "With the system Kilbarry has, Mercer won't be able to check her out easily, and his vetting will be superficial—hopefully. The yacht will be in Kinsale a few more weeks, and Mercer talked about adding hostesses for a photo shoot. She should have enough time to do some snooping."

Declan didn't know Flaherty, and despite her credentials and high marks, he was concerned about her lack of experience in undercover work. She would be on her own with no support system, unable to communicate quickly in an emergency.

Later that day, as Declan was traveling to Cork, Garda Brenda Flaherty, who would be using the name Brenda Delaney, had arrived in Cork District. She was carefully studying plans of the *Fancy Fran* with a naval architect.

It didn't take long for Declan to realize that Brenda Flaherty, a.k.a. Delaney, would be no pushover for the likes of Henson. She was small and hard, with a few soft spots in the right places; bright, penetrating eyes and a keen intellect. She looked good in her uniform, but Declan pictured her as looking even better in the *Fancy*

Fran hostess togs. Her Belfast accent would be obvious to anyone, but details in her backstory would take care of that.

"I think Scarlet Kelly was killed onboard the yacht and freighted out to deeper water in the small boat. The details are in the file. Unfortunately, we found no DNA evidence nor do we have a motive for the killing. Kelly had lyminiol in her system, and we just learned that three others on the boat, including Henson, have records for previous drug-trafficking convictions. It's small stuff, but Interpol has anecdotal information that all may be involved in lyminiol manufacturing and distribution. The FBI in the States also has Henson in their files."

"The yacht would afford good cover for moving drugs, but they would need some very sophisticated hiding places," said Brenda. "Also, I have to tell you. Dogs don't do well at sniffing out lyminiol, unfortunately."

"I've seen Henson and Enda McDonough having dinner together with lady friends in Scilly," Declan said. "I doubt this relationship is strictly casual. I'm thinking he has business dealings with Enda, so watch out for McDonough surfacing in your investigation. His picture is in the file."

Declan set up communication protocols with Brenda. She was given a mobile phone with inconsequential data on it, except for a contact labeled Mother. She was told to text "Red" to this number if she needed to be pulled out immediately and "Green" if everything was copacetic. She could also communicate by wearing something red or green if she was on deck without a phone. Routine communication would be face-to-face with Garda Daly, Brannigan's mate from Kinsale Station, when Brenda could come ashore on errands or downtime. It was thought that Daly would not be known to anyone from the yacht.

When Brenda reported to the yacht at the appointed time, she was wearing a mid-length skirt, which was tight enough to make any deckhand's head turn. A middle-aged woman called Mary O took her in tow. Mary reviewed a list of items on a clipboard with three young women, including Brenda. The prospective hostesses were asked questions, and notes were made on the clipboard.

"Mr. Mercer will make the final determination on your hire, but as far as I can see, you all make the grade."

The girls were paraded into Mercer's office, introduced, and asked to turn revealingly. Con Mercer looked each up and down, dutifully ogled, and made a note on Mary's clipboard. All the girls were acceptable.

Measurements for uniform were taken, and all girls were assigned to the same stateroom.

Mary O said, "We'll not be putting out to sea for this gig, so you won't need to spend much time in here. Use the stateroom for changing and freshening up. There's a locker and bunk for each of you. Meet me on the fore deck in ten minutes."

Outside the girls were introduced to Doug Henson, who turned out to be every bit as ugly as Brenda expected. Mary O was citing her "rules of the road" with respect to service, punctuality, meals, breaks, and decorum.

She then warned, "There will be guys who will paw you and want your full measure of devotion, so to speak. The old ones are the worst. Learn how to handle this without making a big commotion. If things get out of hand, call Mr. Henson."

The yacht normally scheduled about two events a day while in port: public relations, business meetings, entertainment parties. There was plenty of downtime for the hostesses, who could go ashore on these occasions if they could cajole a crew member to transport them in the small boat, or on a launch. There were also scheduled trips ashore for supplies etc. Mercer made a practice of using local hires, so many times the hostesses were met by friends or relatives. Sometimes there were pay-to-play parties, but mostly Mercer Enterprises footed the bill.

Brannigan interrogated Fran Mercer when she returned from Madrid. Fran said Scarlet Kelly was a "nice girl" with whom she had good relations, but she knew nothing about her private life.

Eventually, Brenda got to know Fran, and the two got on well. She was able to learn that Scarlet was not that "nice" and could "wrap Con around her little finger." Fran also confided that she knew nothing about Scarlet's death, but that, if she was murdered, it wouldn't surprise Fran. "She was a thief and tried to steal a piece of my jewelry." Fran even showed the brooch to Brenda and said Doug Henson rescued it from Scarlet when he confronted her in the galley, but she provided no details.

Brenda met with Garda Daly at the designated location in Kinsale. She used Daly's mobile to contact Declan. She told Declan about her discussion with Fran and Henson's return of the brooch.

"Brenda, that puts Henson in the galley with Scarlet Kelly just before she was stabbed with a knife that probably came from the galley," Declan said.

"That brooch copy might have microscopic blood evidence on it. Maybe I should try to steal it for the lab and return it later," she said.

"Too dangerous," Declan said. "Stick to looking for drugs. We can't run the risk of tipping your hand."

CHAPTER 12

S arah Benjamin was not very Jewish in the sense of being a "religious" person, but she did consider heritage and culture important. Her great-great-grandparents were killed in the Holocaust, and she reverently kept a framed picture of them on the wall of the office in her second-floor art gallery on Oliver Plunkett Street in Cork. She was known locally as a promoter of Irish artists, always looking for the traditional Celtic elements which might be lurking in the works of the "undiscovered."

Sarah's parents had been good friends with JJ Foley, who had bought Sham Rock in Kinsale and who shared their interest in fine art. Sarah's parents started the gallery in Cork back in the days when the Irish government was very supportive of artists and building permits were easier to obtain. It was natural for Sarah to develop a close friendship with Bob Foley since they were compatible souls about the same age and grew up developing similar interests. Bob joined the US Navy after college, and Sarah the EDF Irish Ranger Wing.

Sarah married a fellow Ranger, whom she met on a training deployment to Africa. Her husband was subsequently sent with a joint task force of American and EDF units to rescue a stolen North Korean nuclear weapon taken to Chad. The detonator was thought to be separate from the suitcase-size devise, but this turned out to be faulty intelligence. The bomb was ignited and took out hundreds of acres and caused major earthquakes. No one on the task force survived.

A picture of Sarah's husband was eventually placed next to her Holocaust relatives, and it took more than a year for Sarah to find closure. She had no children and threw herself into reaching out to young artists and expanding the gallery.

Working with an electronics company, Sarah developed a unique business model, which eventually spread throughout Europe. The idea was to display copies of original art in hotels, banks, hospitals, offices—all sorts of business establishments. Using their decoration budgets, these client hosts would buy or rent standard-sized framed LED glass panels with built-in power and logic pack. Several pieces of original art could be digitized and loaded to the pack, allowing the displayed work to automatically change at preset intervals. Anyone viewing the art who wanted to buy an original work or commission new work from the artist could do so by contacting the gallery.

Bob Foley had contacted Sarah last year when he came to Kinsale at the start of his building rehab project. He knew from e-mails he had sent that she was very busy traveling around the continent. They wanted to get together for a long time but couldn't seem to connect for one reason or other. Finally, it seemed to be happening. Bob and Sarah decided to have dinner in Cork, see a play, and spend some time together.

It turned out to be a gloomy, rainy evening; but despite the wet, the cold, and the mist, Sarah was radiant. They seemed to waft about in a bubble, conscious of one another's company and little else. For a woman in her fifties, Sarah was beautifully toned. It was obvious her time in the Rangers stood her in good stead. Her face showed the delicate lines of approaching seniority.

They had a lot of catching up to do, but the senses were flooded, and it would take some time to sort it all out.

Bob explained that he had met his old friend, Declan, who was working a case in Kinsale. Sarah thought she might have known Declan but had not followed the news about the murder. He said Declan's daughter, Caitlin, was dating his son, Jim, and that Sarah would have to get acquainted.

Sarah said her sister, Deb, whom Bob remembered vaguely, was all the family she had left in Ireland, her parents having retired to Israel years earlier. Deb would have been a baby when he knew Sarah ages ago. Deb was now a landscape designer who worked with several nurseries, one of which was in Kinsale.

"That's interesting, Sarah," Bob said. "I'm going to be looking for a landscape design for the Rock. Maybe Deb could send me some examples of her work."

Sarah said she would tell Deb and gave Deb's business card to Bob. Of course, she said her little sister was quite good.

Sarah cautiously asked Bob if he was currently seeing anyone, and Bob said he was not connecting in that department. Bob explained that his son, Jim, tried to set him up on a few occasions with some of his older confederates from Ocean Tech, but it was always a disaster.

"How about you, Sarah?" said Bob.

"The last guy I dated wanted to be a copartner in the gallery," she said. "Unfortunately, he brought nothing to the table, and it turned out to be a bad scene."

Sarah wanted Bob to see her gallery and joked about taking him to see her "etchings." The gallery was closed, and their footsteps resonated as they climbed the narrow stairs, close together. He suddenly turned, pressed her to the wall, and kissed her on the mouth. She kissed him back.

"I'm sorry, Sarah," Bob said. "I shouldn't take advantage of our friendship like that."

"Frankly, I was hoping it was more than my etchings you wanted to see, but we'll take it a step at a time," she said and laughed.

The gallery was a large room with several skylights, now dark with the night sky. The lighting was indirect, and small spotlights carefully placed to highlight the paintings on each side wall and the sculpture in the center of the space. At the end of the room, Sarah's office and a storage space were accessible from doors in the back wall. Sarah's gallery was nothing like the virtual art studios and internet graphics shops on the continent, full of electronic wizardry and artificial-intelligence controllers. Sarah said it made her ill just to walk through such places. People hadn't changed since the Renaissance and didn't need to strap on headgear and special sensors to appreciate art.

"I have something I want to show you from the old days," Sarah said. She pointed to two small portraits on the wall of her office: one in charcoal, primitive but promising; the other in oil, bright and modern. Both were portraits of Sarah. "You did the charcoal when you were fourteen, Bob. JJ did the oil."

"I remember doing that. That was just before the family left for the States," said Bob. "That was a great excuse for just staring at you and struggling to keep my testosterone in check."

"I can't say I didn't enjoy being the center of attention. JJ's portrait wasn't as much fun. He took a photo and finished using that as his reference." Sarah pretended to pose, laughing at the soft drama in the vicissitudes of life and the passage of time. "You were a promising artist, and JJ's tutelage was apparent," she said.

"It's a funny thing," said Bob. "JJ, my adopted father, and I had similar talents, but there was obviously no genetic connection. But according to JJ, my birth father was also an artist."

"What do you know about your birth father?" Sarah asked.

Bob was suddenly pensive.

"Virtually nothing, except his being an artist," he said. "JJ gave me an old photo before he died. There was no name or date, but 'Graystone' was written on the back. It was a picture of a young man in an open collar shirt, who looked like me except for a full beard. I have it back at the Rock. I'll show it to you when you come to look at *my* etchings."

Bob explained that he didn't think about his birth father, whose name was never given to him by JJ, assuming JJ even knew it.

"JJ was all the dad I needed or wanted," he said.

"What about your mother, Bob?" Sarah asked.

"I have no photos of her and know nothing about her," said Bob. "So, you see. I'm a man of mystery. I might even be Jewish. Wouldn't that make your sister and parents happy if we were to hook up?"

"They wouldn't give a damn, Bob. But they might be curious about your presumptuousness," Sarah said.

The banter went on for a while until Bob wasn't paying much attention. He was watching Sarah bathed in the light from the overhead spot and imagining that she was a life-size clay Venus, still being molded by the sculptor's hands—his hands—wet with slip and sensuously driven around each curve, pushing and kneading, patting and firming.

"Do you still have anything to do with the Rangers, Sarah?" Bob asked.

"Yeah. My old unit meets for breakfast every month, and we trade stories. It's all great fun until I start getting asked if I'm seeing anyone," she said. "Then occasionally I get referrals to 'art lovers,' who are also 'single.' I'm never sure what one has to do with the other."

Sarah quickly changed the subject to her LED frames project. She said she hoped Bob was continuing with his watercolor/colored-pencil portrait work and that they would make interesting additions to her gallery.

"Wouldn't it be interesting to see portraits of the same person, changing in the frame every five minutes or so, a different pose each time?"

CHAPTER 13

During a meeting with Daly on shore in Kinsale, Garda Brenda Flaherty (Delaney) had a strong feeling that someone was watching them. She expressed her sense of this to Daly and suggested that they needed to find a different meeting place.

When Brenda returned to the yacht, she found that her mobile was missing from her locker. She was contemplating her situation when the stateroom door was rapped several times. She was apprehensive because she knew the other girls assigned to the stateroom wouldn't have bothered to knock.

Doug Henson entered, holding her mobile, and said, "I found this on the foredeck, Delaney. Your name was on the phone contact list. You shouldn't be so careless."

"I don't carry that outside," she said. "There's no place on our uniforms to put it."

"Like I said, Delaney, don't be so careless.'"

Doug threw the mobile on the bunk and left with a grimace, half concealed in the scars on his face.

Brenda knew that Henson had been all through the phone, probably calling some of the prop numbers and checking the photo gallery. Things were getting too close for comfort. He might have been suspicious, but he didn't know anything for certain. If that was the case, she probably would have been taken on a boat ride like Scarlet Kelly, one she wouldn't return from.

Brenda also knew that some of the other girls complained about "being followed." They just wrote it off to voyeurs, but Brenda knew they were all being checked out. Either something triggered this, or Mercer and company were being extra cautious. Still, compared to the other hostesses, Brenda stood out as being extra cool and savvy. She wasn't all that great in the acting department and suspected that she would be at the top of Henson's list if he was looking for an undercover cop.

It didn't take Brenda long to realize that there were only two places on the yacht that would make good drug-hiding places if they were stored in any large quantity, even given the fact that the boat was over one hundred meters long.

The first was the galley storage locker, where they could be disguised as some kind of grocery item. This would probably require the complicity of the cook, Bertha Maloney, and Brenda was sure she wouldn't have anything to do with drugs.

The second possibility was inside one of the large battery cell storage units. Brenda's discussion with the naval architect in Cork led her to believe that three storage units would be more than adequate for a vessel the size of Mercer's yacht, but the *Fancy Fran* had four. They were not able to find any legitimate outfitting record of modifications, and apparently, no red flags resulted from any maritime safety inspections. Brenda waited to get better intelligence from Daly during one of their meetings, but the district had nothing to pass along.

Henson was getting increasingly suspicious. Part of his concern stemmed from the fact that Mercer's trust of Henson was fraying ever since he botched the disposal of Scarlet Kelly's body. Henson had to prove his reliability and worth to the enterprise more than ever, what with the Gardai impounding the small boat, watching activities on the yacht more closely, and digging into the files on Mercer and his employees. Another slip could be fatal.

Brenda decided she would get into the good graces of one of the engine crew. The deckhands/engineers were a solitary lot, often excluded from the topside party activities and "good times." One in particular, Rory Clay, seemed the young and impressionable type, who would probably succumb to Brenda's charms given the right opportunity. Captain Syl Thornberg also served as chief engineer, but his right-hand man was definitely Rory Clay who handled everything from failing storage cells to backed-up plumbing.

The rest of the crew were older, several married with families. This made Rory a loner who usually had to scrounge for a drinking buddy when he was off duty. Usually, he would spend his idle time working out on a mat near his assigned station below deck or cadging leftovers from the cook, Bertha. Bertha liked Rory and thought of him as the son she could have had but now never would. Brenda thought to take advantage of this relationship.

As an ex-Special Forces Ranger and Gardai drug officer, Brenda was no stranger to weekly workouts. She approached Bertha about finding a place to exercise which would be away from the lascivious, prying eyes of some of the male crew. There was a workout room set aside for crew and staff, but Brenda lied that she preferred someplace more private. Most people concentrating on physical exercise don't pay much attention to the other exercisers, but this would not occur to Bertha, who saw an opportunity for her "son" to hook up with a beautiful, intelligent woman. She eagerly suggested Brenda might share Rory's workout space.

Rory was pleased to share space and even equipment with Brenda. He literally brightened when Brenda was in his company and felt—with no little justification—that he moved up a few pegs in the esteem of others in the engineering crew.

It wasn't long before Brenda was navigating the confines of the engineering space with hardly anyone taking notice. Even Doug Henson seemed to relax and accept the happier thought that maybe Rory Clay finally got lucky.

Brenda took advantage of her newfound access and asked Rory to explain the intricacies of the power, hydraulics, and electronics systems. She smiled a lot and presented the image of a rapt student, in suppliance before a wondrous, all-knowing instructor. Of course, the elements of sexual attraction were never far below the surface, and Brenda was very good at playing this card.

Her assumption was correct that the fourth energy storage cell was a dummy, or rather a space being put to other purpose. Rory confirmed that it was not tied in to the other cells and was, in fact, a secure space under the strict control of the security officer, Doug Henson. Rory didn't know what it was used for and didn't want to know so long as Henson and a few of his goons made it clear that this was a prohibited area.

Pretending naivete, Brenda tried the access hatch and found it locked. A tap on the side of the tight metal mesh proved that the cell wasn't hollow and, given its size, could have contained thousands of kilos of anything—maybe contraband. Rory hung back from the cell and suggested Brenda do the same.

High up on the bulkhead in the corner of the energy cell space, a tiny video camera surveyed the area. The digital images were piped to a console in Doug Henson's stateroom on the main deck, forward. Brenda was unaware of the video cam, and Rory never thought about it. Henson reviewed the pictures about once daily when he was onboard and occasionally deleted the images to conserve file space.

When Henson reviewed the video footage the following afternoon, his worst fears were confirmed. Brenda Delaney was a plant, and if she would have gotten into that cell, she would be a real threat. So far, she hasn't seen the drugs; but if she's an undercover cop, she likely already called her contact, and a search warrant is underway. He couldn't bet on the fact that Mercer's political contacts would shut down a possible raid or search. The goods had to be moved to a safe location as soon as possible.

Henson called Enda McDonough and told him to get ready to receive a shipment that night. Enda said the crypt wasn't ready yet, but he had another secure spot that would work temporarily.

"You better make sure it's secure, shithead," said Henson.

He then called two of his cronies and told them to load one of the launches with cases of coffee capsules from the galley storage locker and tarp them over. He then paged Brenda on the ship's PA.

"We won't need your services anymore, Delaney. Go see Mary O and pickup your final payment," he said.

"What's going on, Mr. Henson?

"You were nosing around in off-limits areas. I've got you on video cam. Now I want you outta here," Henson said. "You have fifteen minutes to get your gear in that launch. And leave your uniform on the bunk."

Brenda went to her shared stateroom and quickly put on a red outfit. She grabbed her mobile, clicked on Mother, and texted, "Coming home with packages. Meet me at dock."

The motor launch was met by Brannigan and Daly, warrant in hand, who told the crew to remove the tarp and open one of the cases.

"That's a lot of coffee, boys. No coffee drinkers on the *Fancy Fran*? Hard to believe," Brannigan said.

"The stuff doesn't come up to Mr. Mercer's standards. We're returning it to the supplier," the crewman said.

"Let's check it out," Brannigan said, slitting open one of the cups and sniffing and tasting the contents. "Yup. That's coffee."

"What were you expecting?" sneered the crewman, "Gardai Station sewage? You ought to be familiar with that."

"Well, I'm always looking for something better. But that's not it. Where are you hiding the good stuff?" Brannigan waved them off, and they puttered to another landing.

Brenda was not paying much attention to the banter. She grabbed her gear and headed for the wharf-side pub, visibly upset. In fact, she was furious that she had been played and humiliated. Her chance to bring down Mercer and company had, to her mind, ignominiously failed.

On another occasion, her red dress might have attracted the attentions of some rovers in the pub. This time, they were warned off by a scowling face that would have blistered battleship paint. Brenda was in no mood for small talk when Declan McGuinness appeared in the doorway.

CHAPTER 14

Declan smiled and handed Brenda a whiskey and soda.

"It's early for this, but I think you need it, Brenda. We'll get them. It will just take a little longer. You flushed them out, and that means they'll have to change their business model. That's got to be a huge disruption."

"I could have gotten into that storage cell, Mac," said Brenda. "I thought I had more time. And I should have spotted that video cam."

"We wouldn't be here talking if you did," said Declan.

"Don't sell me short, Mac. I'm no Scarlet Kelly. If he tried something on me, I'd break his arm in two places."

Brenda swigged the whiskey and asked for another.

Declan had no doubt that Garda Brenda Flaherty, a.k.a. Delaney, ex-Special Forces, could have done a lot of damage. He was also fairly sure she wouldn't have made it out alive. But this was not the time to disabuse her of her second thoughts.

"Brenda, I have one piece of news to share. You may or may not like it, but I'm thinking you will like it." Declan paused diplomatically. "The superintendent wanted you to return to Dublin, but I convinced him you would want to see this through and I would have your back. He agreed to you staying on the case for now."

Brenda visibly lit up and said, "You're a genius, Mac. That's exactly what I want. You knew that." She hugged him then blushed and tucked into her drink.

"We have to talk about what comes next," said Declan. "A guy by the name of Enda McDonough is Doug Henson's contact man in Kinsale. He's the guy who found Scarlet Kelly's body, but he claimed he didn't know her. I want you to spend some time with McDonough and find out what you can. He's not the killer, but I'll bet he knows who is."

"Henson will have to get those drugs—which I'm convinced he has—off the yacht as soon as he can. It's likely he would use a contact in Kinsale to take receipt and hide them." Brenda lowered her eyes. "So what's my backstory?"

"You're a reporter from RTE, doing a piece on Scarlet Kelly," said Declan. He handed her a set of phony credentials. "We've cleared it with RTE who will route any inquiry about you to one of our people. Your pseudonym will be Brenda Carter. Contact me on the same mobile you had on the yacht if you need, but be careful."

Declan said he had to go to Cork to go over Mercer's Interpol file with a guy from Brussels.

"We booked you a room at the Upton, so you won't have to bunk in the back room of Kinsale Station next to Sergeant Twomey's orchid plants. Have a good meal and check out McDonough in the file. Get to see him tonight and watch his shenanigans in case he tries to pick up any shipments."

Declan wished her good luck and spun out the door. Brenda thanked him and decided she would waste no time in checking out the availability of Enda McDonough.

Brenda caught McDonough returning from a funeral in Riverstick. She identified herself and said she was doing a story on Scarlet Kelly, talking to everyone Scarlet knew. Interestingly, Enda didn't deny he knew Scarlet. She asked if he would have dinner with her at Murphy's Pub, and he accepted at once. First, he said he would have to see to his mother's care, and a time was arranged.

Brenda's impression of Enda McDonough was off-putting when he approached her table in the pub. She thought that for someone coming from a funeral, he was excessively disheveled.

"A sad occasion, Mr. McDonough. How well did you know the deceased?"

"I went to school with her, but we haven't communicated in many years. I can't say I really knew her or her family. Still, it's important to make the final goodbye," said Enda. "I go to many funerals. It's when you see people at their finest and most forgiving."

There seemed to be no intended irony in the fact that he really enjoyed funerals.

There was at this time a French women's soccer team in town, and several were at the bar with their boyfriends. They spoke English very well but were slurring their speech and presenting a rowdy distraction. One of the young men dropped his pants, exposing his butt for one and all. The proprietor wasn't watching when a pretty girl in the group bent and planked a big, lipstick-ringed kiss on the swain's ass, probably payment for a lost bet.

In the ensuing melee, Enda's mobile rang—a morose dirge. The mobile was laying on the table, and Brenda could see a name come up: Doug Henson. Enda picked up the device, didn't say much, then put it back on the table.

"Guess I can spend more time with you than I thought. I won't have to run errands tonight."

Actually, Enda didn't know much about Scarlet and seemed to be trying to stretch the conversation. Brenda was doing the same, hoping other tidbits of information, which would help the investigation, might be dropped.

Two plates of stew were delivered to the table along with a bread basket and two frosty mugs of ale. Soon Enda's atrocious table manners were on display, making Brenda think the butt-kissing episode might make for an easier visual.

"You know, Mr. McDonough, you seem to have a fascination for the dark side of things," Brenda said. "Perhaps the effort of caring for your mother is wearing you down."

"Oh, Mum's no problem. I have people who come in. And call me Enda," he said. "Funny you mention the dark side. I just bought an old, empty crypt up at St. Mary's, and I'm having it fixed up for me and Mum for when the time comes. Should be dry as a bone inside when I'm all finished—no pun intended."

Brenda coughed a little and reached for a response, saying, "I'd like to see it when you're finished. I love monuments. Very historical."

She thought two things at this point. First, if Henson were off-loading the drugs from the *Fancy Fran*, he would do it tonight, knowing that the Gardai would be back with a warrant in the morning. Second, this crypt Enda was talking about would make a perfect hiding place, but obviously, it wasn't ready yet. She decided to stick with Enda for the evening to see what he would do. She believed this was also what Mac had in mind, but she would need to share her thoughts about the crypt.

Three pubs later, Enda was feeling no pain and barely able to keep up with Brenda. She had switched to ginger ale two pubs ago and decided, coming out of the Dragon's Head, that Enda needed to be taken home. He stumbled through his doorway, crashed onto a pile of bed-linen laundry at the base of the stairway to his room, and passed out. Brenda waited a few minutes outside the entrance to his house, listening to his snores, and then decided there would be no drug delivery that night. She headed for her room at the Upton.

Captain Syl Thornberg and his crew knew that the *Fancy Fran* occasionally ferried drugs. Except for a few of the deckhands who were Henson's goons, none of the crew touched the stuff, and they pretended it was none of their business. They knew that if drugs or any kind of contraband were found on the yacht, their jobs would be over, and they could be arrested. Privately Syl Thornberg thought lyminiol wasn't a serious drug and should be legal; though he would never take it himself.

Henson didn't want to take the chance that running the drugs over to McDonough could be done safely. He felt sure that the yacht was under surveillance, and besides, he didn't trust Enda to hold up his end. When he called Enda and confirmed that the crypt wasn't ready, he made up his mind that the *Fancy Fran* would have to haul ass earlier than had been scheduled.

Henson knocked on the door to Con Mercer's stateroom, which was adjacent to his own. He found Mercer rolling a wineglass in his hand and shooing a scantily clad hostess into his en suite.

"Sorry to interrupt, Boss, but we can't move the drugs off the *Fran* tonight. Too risky. We need to weigh anchor and head out as soon as possible."

Enraged, Mercer shouted at Henson, "What the fuck did you screw up now! Is this your Scarlet Kelly mistake coming down on us?"

"It's Brenda Delaney. I think she was an undercover cop. They don't know what we got for sure, but they know we're using the storage cell. We can't dump hundreds of thousands of Euros worth of goods into the Bandon River," said Henson.

"Get Syl and his first officer up here now! Roust Mary O and tell her to make the girls an offer. They can leave now, or we'll fly them back from France after we get there. And get word to Frances. Pick her up at the bazaar in town. Jaysus Christ, Registry will have a fit when they find out we're leaving without an escort."

Mercer glowered at Henson.

CHAPTER 15

When illegal drugs became an increasing problem after the formation of the Republic of Europe, the Irish Coast Guard was reorganized as part of the European Defense Force Coast Guard. The mission of maritime safety, pollution prevention, and search and rescue was expanded to include armed intervention of smugglers and coastal defense. EDFCG gunboats were routinely outfitted with HCL guns. These weapons could drill a three-inch, smoldering hole through a vessel with 150-mm plate, but the more-usual practice was to fire a warning into the water ahead of a boat, producing a large cloud of steam.

HCL technology extended to pistols and rifles, and all had adjustable voltage which controlled the caliber, shape, and range of the beam. There was no "stun setting" like the old science-fiction phasers boasted, and the lowest HCL setting would spread a short-range beam and heat the target to 176 degrees Celsius. To stop someone at the lowest setting, an instantaneous blip could be fired, which would leave the target with something akin to a cigarette burn. HCL shots could be deadly accurate because there was no bullet, hence no problem with air resistance or other atmospheric effects.

Normally, the Gardai did not carry firearms; though they were trained to use them if they were needed for special missions. So it was that Brenda and Declan were carrying HCL pistols when they arrived at Cappagh on the morning after Brenda's meeting with Enda McDonough. The yacht, *Fancy Fran*, had left in the night, and they would have to move quickly. Declan alerted the EDFCG so they could follow with backup as needed.

Sergeant Pat Twomey was up on the pad to wish them Godspeed, and he soon became a speck in the rearview of the robo drone. The aircraft headed for the Atlantic, and the sun to the southeast slanted through the polarized, acrylic bubble of the central pod, causing Declan to put on his sunglasses. Brenda was already wearing her glasses, along with an HCL-proof, heat-resistant vest. She was buoyant with the idea of getting Mercer.

The ocean was a sun-speckled blue-gray stripe along the horizon, and the land behind them was receding quickly as the drone's blades spun relentlessly, glistening and purring. Declan's primeval fear of the cold depths of the Atlantic were lessened somewhat by the tiny, comforting image of the prow of the coast guard gunboat cresting in the distance far below. As yet, the *Fancy Fran* could not be seen, and Declan was totally reliant on the tracking ability of the GPS technology.

Suddenly a cold sweat came over Declan as a blue beam came through the floor of the pod and pierced the top of the acrylic dome. It was followed instantly by acrid smoke and the smell of ozone.

A low FFFTH sound was heard, and another blue flash pierced Brenda's arm. She winced in extreme pain and blanched in a silent scream as the smell of burning flesh permeated the cabin space. Her eyes rolled in her head, and she passed out. Declan saw that one of the rotors had been blasted off its arm, and the others tried to automatically compensate to keep the craft from spinning out of control.

Declan saw quickly that Brenda's wound was not bleeding heavily partly due to the fact that the flesh was seared. He hoped an artery had not been hit but knew that it wouldn't be long before the blood flow from the wound would increase. The drone was wheeling in wide circles as it headed toward the dreaded Atlantic at a moderate rate of descent.

Then another blue beam stabbed through the drone, piercing the battery below the pod and exiting the top of the dome. The remaining drone engines slowed with the loss of voltage, and the descent rate increased. Fortunately, the battery was the self-healing type and continued to function at reduced strength. The console, however, had been damaged, and Declan worried that the automatic control would quit, causing the drone to tumble helplessly from the sky. He felt like a wounded pigeon waiting for the coup de grâce.

Declan could tell that the last shot seemed to come from the shore, in the direction of the Old Head of Kinsale. He also thought that the coast guard boat had engaged the shooters and was heading in their direction. This was a distraction for the shooters, and it meant that the drone might suffer no more hits and make it down in one piece. But then what?

The drone continued to descend in wide circles, and Declan saw that Brenda was visibly failing. He was saddened to think that she was the one with the safety vest and was hit anyway. Then he noticed that the vest had also been hit, but not penetrated! She was fortunate after all. She had to make it, he thought, and wrapped her entrance wound with his handkerchief as best as he could.

The drone hit the water hard in a sweeping arc, and the sea, which was a dappled plate from high up, suddenly became a rough, cold, turbulent reality. Briny water spurted through the battery hole and the entire pod and shattered acrylic dome creaked and groaned under the impact of the waves.

Declan feared that the pod would fill with water and sink and that he and Brenda would become fish food. The motors had shut down, but the running lights at the end of the arms were dimly blinking. Brenda was reviving somewhat as a result of the cold, salty water, and she had regained some of her color. Her pulse was low, but she was able to open her eyes briefly, moaning with pain.

He stuffed the hole in the floor of the pod with his socks, and it seemed to do the trick. He then took a plate from the rear of the damaged console and slammed it against the hole in the acrylic dome. It could work, he thought. Then he set his HCL on low and softened the edges of the hole with brief blasts. The acrylic melted into the plate, and a seal was achieved. Declan was unaware that Brenda had been watching him do this, and she was able to utter one word: "Brilliant."

There were about six inches of water on the floor of the pod, but the seats were higher and relatively dry. As the afternoon wore on, the wind died down, and the sea began to calm. The sloshing in the pod and the rolling motion subsided.

Declan thought it might be a good time to open the vent in the top of the pod and get some fresh air now that things had calmed down. He noticed there was blood on the vent handle then realized that it was his. His mouth was salty, and his head was bleeding; must have happened during the hard landing, and he didn't feel it until now.

There was a first-aid kit on the drone, but it was stowed under the console seat. The bandages were dry, and he wrapped Brenda's arm carefully. He traced the line of the wound with his eyes and decided neither the bone nor artery were hit. She was extremely fortunate; though she had lost a lot of blood. The water in the pod was pinkish.

Declan could see dorsal fins circling the drone some distance out. Sharks would be naturally curious about an object in the water and would investigate. He was glad now that he wasn't able to bail out the pod. Tiny amounts of blood in the water could reach a shark's olfactory senses and keep them on the alert, unwilling to leave. If the wind came up, the sea could roughen and break the pod apart. He didn't want to think about what would happen then.

Declan used up much of his HCL charge on the acrylic repair, and the battery was too low to provide much recharge. He could use Brenda's pistol, but if they got separated in the water, she would have no defense. In any case, he preferred not to drain the battery any further in order to keep the running lights flashing as long as possible. Their chances for rescue were slim if no lights could be seen. Also, he wasn't sure how long Brenda could hold out.

Around sunset, the wind picked up, and sharks began slamming into the floor of the pod. All of a sudden, the socks Declan had rammed into the bottom hole disappeared, apparently pulled out from below. He quickly jammed a role of bandages from the first-aid kit into the hole but guessed that some bloody water had already escaped the pod.

The banging on the pod continued, and the sea started to get rougher. Suddenly a loud horn sounded, and a spotlight probed the dark and lit up the inside of the dome.

"Thank God."

Declan sighed and gave Brenda a hug.

The pod hatch wouldn't open, so the two volunteers from the Royal National Lifeboat Institution pried it apart, wrapped Declan and Brenda in blankets, and removed them to an inflatable craft bobbing close by. A tow was put on the drone, and they sped to a waiting updated Severn-class lifeboat.

Following examination by a doctor on board the lifeboat, Declan was taken below and given a hot cup of soup. Brenda was taken to an operating table. Her wound was dressed, and she was hooked up to an IV.

"The coast guard got into a firefight with the guys that shot your drone down," the RNLI skipper said. "They called us in to help out with the rescue. I'm glad we spotted your lights. It saved a lot of time."

"And our lives," said Declan, rubbing his head.

CHAPTER 16

Declan called his daughter, Caitlin, to tell her he was hurt on the job and was returning to Dublin for a week's rest and medical examination. He tried to assure her it was nothing serious, but she was instantly suspicious. He was not going to stop by to see her but would visit her when he returned in a week or so. She decided to call Sergeant Pat Twomey and try to inveigle more information.

"He was hurt in the line of duty, darlin'," Twomey said. "A bump on the head. Nothing serious, but the Gardai always wants to make sure everything is carefully checked."

That made Caitlin even more suspicious, and she decided to call her father's good friend and Jim's father, Bob Foley, to see what he could share.

Bob measured his words cautiously because he wasn't sure how much Declan would want Caitlin to know.

"Dec's drone had rotor problems," he said. "He had to make an emergency landing in the Atlantic and bumped his head as a result. You know how your father hates the ocean, but fortunately, he and his partner, Garda Brenda Flaherty, were quickly rescued by the RNLI. Brenda hurt her arm, and she's in hospital in Kinsale."

"Damn the Irish! You never can get a straight story," blurted Caitlin.

"I'm sure he didn't want you to worry, Caitlin. Don't be too hard on him." Bob tried to change the subject and was finally successful. "What's going on with you and Jim? He was supposed to visit with Con Mercer days ago, and now Mercer's yacht has departed."

"Jim told me his meeting was postponed, but apparently, Mercer is still interested in doing business with Ocean Tech."

Caitlin said she was meeting with Jim for dinner; after which he was taking her out to his project on the River Lee.

"Well, you two be careful. I don't know if I'd want to be out on the River Lee at night," Bob said. "But on one side, you could say it's a cheap date."

"Bob. Tell me. Do you think I should visit Brenda Flaherty in the hospital?"

"No, absolutely not." Bob could see that Caitlin was still exploring for ways to get more information about her father. "Leave Brenda to the comfort of her relatives. Don't be going there to rake over coals. Dec will give you all the details of his 'accident' when he's ready."

Caitlin thanked Bob, wished him well, and returned the mobile to her pocket. She toyed with the idea of calling her mother in Dublin but decided against it. She realized she would be rationing information to her mother exactly as had been done to her.

She went through her day totally distracted with thoughts of Brenda and her father involved in some horrific police operation. She knew he had been called down from Dublin for something "special." What was he doing, flying in a drone out into the Atlantic? Caitlin looked at her students' faces as if they were dream images. She couldn't wait for the recess bell, and finally, it came. She was soon alone again with her thoughts and decided to call the hospital in Kinsale.

"Brenda Flaherty was transferred to St. James's Hospital in Dublin this morning. I can give you the number," the voice on the line said.

Caitlin called and was transferred by the front desk to another number.

A woman answered, "Siobhan Reilly, Burns Unit. Can I help you?"

"This is Caitlin McGuinness. I'm a close friend of Brenda Flaherty. Can you tell me if she's receiving visitors?"

"I'm afraid not, ma'am. Check again tomorrow. But if you're not a relative, I think it will be a while before you get to see her."

Caitlin could not get any more specifics, so the call ended. She suddenly thought she would send some flowers to Brenda with a note from "the McGuinness family." Whatever was wrong with Brenda, it sounded like she got the worst end of the situation.

She assumed that Brenda had somehow been badly burned in the drone crash but couldn't comprehend how that could happen. There was no flammable fuel on a drone, and the newer, high-capacity drone batteries could be punctured and wet without igniting. It was all very mysterious to Caitlin. Maybe Jim could shed some light on things when she saw him that evening.

Caitlin showered after work and studied herself in the mirror. She was a tall, beautiful woman who could stand toe to toe with Jim Foley. In fact, on several occasions she showered with Jim and stood next to him with their noses and genitals touching, letting the steamy water course the outside while the juices of passion surged within.

A long strip of violet clouds hung over the River Lee as Caitlin greeted Jim Foley on the quay. Jim wanted to eat at one of the restaurants near the English Market, but he didn't want to stray too far from the river. An Ocean Tech boat would be waiting for them when they finished, and things could get slippery on the dock if the clouds let loose a torrent of rain. Besides, a long walk in a summer rain might sound romantic but in Ireland would be a chilly reminder of the latitude.

Years ago, the River Lee was a receptacle for all kinds of sewage. The Irish government, with help from the EU, spent millions building civil works and treatment plants to help clean it up. Recycling and waste discipline contributed greatly to improvement. The water-level rise brought on by climate change helped with dispersal, but brought problems of its own. Eventually, water levels receded toward historic markers and fish life returned.

Companies like Ocean Technologies Inc. saw opportunities for investment in an English-speaking country with a well-educated population and a water system that had the perfect parameters for the kind of aquaculture they wanted to develop. Temperatures, chemistry, and biology had to be just right, and the River Lee fit the bill.

After dining, Caitlin and Jim walked quickly for the OT boat when the sky cut loose with a torrent of large drops. Both were prepared, and their umbrellas collided when they opened them at the same time. Laughing, they stepped into a covered areaway and decided to let the worst of the weather pass.

"Jim, do you think my father is involved in something dangerous?" Caitlin said.

"Well, he is investigating a murder. Of course, he's done that plenty in his career. I wouldn't worry, Caitlin."

Jim didn't make any connection with Mercer and knew none of the details of Declan's investigation. Their banter soon changed to the weather, and the darkening skies began to light up with a splash of moonlight on the gray clouds. They shook out their umbrellas and continued toward the dock.

The electric motor on the OT boat took a while to start. Some moisture had apparently shorted connections. Eventually, it turned over, and they started down the Lee toward the site of Jim's project.

A long row of three lines extended for hundreds of meters in the direction of the current, each marked and anchored to the river bottom about every three meters. Four horizontal lines tied to the uprights ran underwater at different depths, parallel to each other and the top lines. The deepest line was encrusted with coral polyps, the next with clams, the second from the top with mussels, and the uppermost with a luxuriant growth of kelp. All this aquaculture was grown and monitored as part of OT's River Lee project.

"I'm especially proud of the coral, Caitlin," Jim said. "Not only can it thrive in fresh or brackish water at this latitude and with this composition but it—along with the kelp—gobbles up tons of dissolved carbon dioxide."

"I suppose you're going to tell me that everything but the coral is edible?" she said.

"Of course," said Jim. "We harvest it routinely and, in fact, sell some of it at the English market. It's perfectly safe and delicious."

Jim Foley had a doctorate in marine biology, but his special passion was restoration and expansion of coral beds. He held several patents for cultures that would provide a range of benefits and characteristics but most of all facilitate the development and sustainability of all kinds of other marine life.

The moon was slipping behind more rain clouds when Jim and Caitlin decided to return to the more-familiar, warmer, and dryer comforts of Caitlin's apartment. The following day's agenda was on each of their minds when they decided to call it a night.

CHAPTER 17

Following a week in France, Con Mercer returned to his native Libya, home of Mercer Enterprises Inc. and headquarters for several of his companies.

This was not the Libya of 2011, the cartoonish desert kingdom of scrappy warlords and impoverished hordes. Libya had hundreds of miles of beautiful Mediterranean coastline, a warm climate, and lots of real estate, albeit mostly desert. Eventually, following years of bloody fighting, a cadre of smart, practical leaders put in place a framework of good governance and productive alliances. The country prospered under a right-leaning, democratic government. The thousands of sub-Saharan Africans that used to crowd the beaches, trying to migrate to Europe, suddenly found employment, shelter, and safety on the African side. A huge aquifer was discovered in the center of the country and, along with solar-powered desalinization plants and international investment, soon made large swathes of the country green.

The manufacture and sale of lyminiol was legal in Libya, though highly regulated, and Mercer owned a small manufacturing facility which produced fully a third of the world's supply. His lyminiol was pure and high quality and distributed both legally and illegally to hundreds of distribution points around the globe. Inevitably, his product would be adulterated with all kinds of material, but this didn't bother him. Addiction or death by poisoning or overdose were not Mercer's concerns. Lyminiol also had medical uses, but it was all the same to Mercer. A smooth-running universe which added to his bottom line was the only ideology that motivated him.

The Interpol had paid a visit to his yacht and found his extra energy cell full of coffee from Mercer's own plantation, ground and packaged in small plastic cups. Mercer was grateful that Henson had warned him about the energy cell but also upset that his screwup led to the focus on the cell in the first place. Henson made returning to Kinsale anytime soon a difficult proposition, but return he must. The Saudi prince who wanted to invest in his desert project was also an avid shark fisherman, and Kinsale was a world center for such. Mercer had promised to take him there and introduce him to the right people. But not right now.

Mercer had to meet with Dr. Jim Foley from Ocean Tech. He had to postpone meeting with him earlier in Kinsale because of all the trouble surrounding the Scarlet Kelly incident, but he couldn't delay any longer. He needed access to OT's special algae for his desert project and needed to convince them that a contract with Mercer would be to their mutual benefit.

He decided it would be better to fly Foley to Tripoli and get him out to some of the prospective sites in the desert. Nothing like a hands-on touchy-feely to get the brain cells working. 65 percent of the earth's land surface was either desert or undergoing desertification, and this, after substantial progress, had been made in slowing or halting the process in many areas. Foley's algae could withstand thirty- to forty-degree Celsius daytime and zero-degree night temperatures, but how would it get moisture? Mercer's Libyan, Chinese, and Arabian backers would need answers. They wanted a viable, economical carbon sequestration offset to their natural gas exploration plans. OT was his best hope.

The letter Mercer sent to the CEO of OT specifically requested the services of Dr. Jim Foley and included a packet of information and an open reservation on a charter flight to Tripoli. In-country accommodations and travel arrangements would be taken care of. Doug Henson would meet Jim Foley at the airport.

The executives at OT jumped at the opportunity to engage in a project with Mercer Enterprises, despite Mercer's shady reputation. They told Jim, however, that a lawyer from their legal department, Anne Baker, would accompany Jim to assist with contractual matters. Mercer had no objection; though privately he would have preferred someone with more of a scientific background.

Jim told Caitlin of his planned trip and said it should last about a week. Caitlin's interest piqued when Jim mentioned he would be traveling with Anne Baker, a company attorney. She checked out Anne Baker on the OT website and was dismayed to find out that she was an attractive blonde in her thirties. When she told this to Jim, his interest also piqued. He assumed spending a week with an attorney would be a bore. Now things were picking up.

When Anne Baker settled down opposite Jim on the charter plane, she indeed held out the prospect of an interesting trip. Anne liked martinis, book clubs, and skeet-shooting. She grew up in Baltimore, Maryland, and was surprised to learn there was a town with the same name on the southern coast of Ireland.

"So how did you wind up with this assignment, Anne?" Jim asked.

"Strictly by default," said Anne. "One of my older colleagues was picked, but his wife had a heart attack the next day, so he had to bail."

"Well, as my grandfather used to say, 'It's an ill wind that doesn't blow someone some good.'" Jim thought Anne looked fit but also suspected she was more accustomed to urban landscapes. "You'll probably be traveling with me out to a few desert locations. Hope you're up for that."

"Mercer will make sure we're taken care of. After all, we are his meal ticket, or at least you are."

Anne was probably right, and they wouldn't have too much walking to do.

Henson was at the airport terminal when they arrived in Tripoli. They welcomed the conditioned air after being enveloped in a wave of heat. Henson greeted Jim Foley with a strange question.

"You are the son of Robert Foley who is renovating a house in Scilly?"

"Yes," Jim said quizzically. "And you are Doug Henson, Mercer's head of security?" Then, to lighten the occasion, he added, "Son of Mr. Henson?"

Henson wasn't amused and quickly switched to business.

"We have arranged transportation to the Madrigal Arms where you will be staying. A driver will pick you up in the morning at 0900 hours to take you to Mr. Mercer's yacht for a breakfast meeting. You are free for the rest of the day. Enjoy the facilities." Then on a very slightly friendlier note, he added, "Welcome to Libya."

The Madrigal Arms was a large, modern structure, gleaming white concrete interspersed with large panes of darkened glass. Henson left them in the lobby after they checked in, and they repaired to the lounge while their bags were delivered to the rooms.

It took over seven hours to fly from Cork, and dinner and cocktails were appropriate to the encroaching evening hour.

Anne was starting to sip her third martini of the day when she offered, "That was a strange and scary man. He must be good at what he does. I don't see a whole lot going for him."

"I don't think he knows my father," said Jim, "but he seems to have some kind of interest in him."

Following a meal of layered potato and ground lamb, known locally as mubattan kusha, Anne and Jim were finishing up with sweet tea and semolina cakes. The bar was lined with patrons sipping Western-style cocktails.

Anne asked, "How are you planning to package this deal, Dr. Foley—Jim?"

"Well, according to the packet his company worked up, he wants to do three plots of about two hundred acres each, using our new strain 682B algae. This should remove the tonnage of carbon dioxide he needs for the trade, provided we solve the moisture problem," Jim said.

"I can't help you with that. It looks like a simple-enough transaction," Anne said, "but we need to indemnify the company if your moisture arrangement doesn't work out. I'm not sure how to do that until I see what you have in mind."

Anne put on her distance glasses and scanned the bar.

"You see that attractive, dark gal at the end of the bar? I'm going to be spending the night with her," she said. "Sorry, Jim. You're not the right type or gender." At that, she started to leave.

Jim was startled but quickly grasped what was happening.

"Wait," he said. "You don't know her. That could be dangerous."

"Don't worry. I can tell you she is gay and an agent of Interpol. That information is conveyed by each of the two lapel pins she's wearing. I'm wearing one of those pins myself. See?" Anne pointed to a small, heart-shaped pink pin dangling on a gold neck chain.

"The education process never ends," Jim said. "I should have suspected when you didn't try to rub my knee under the table." Both laughed.

"Seriously," he said. "Pickups can be risky. Leave me a text with your location just in case I have to come get you at 0900."

Chapter 18

Anne was wearing dark glasses and moving very slowly when she met Jim in the morning.

"Sorry, Jim. I should have heeded your warning. That gal was way ahead of me in the drink department. Still, I did learn that she and her mates just completed an inspection of Mercer's yacht—looking for drugs, no less. They didn't find any but thought it unusual that an empty energy cell was being used for coffee storage."

"There should be plenty of coffee for your 'morning after' recuperation, Anne," Jim said, "but I suggest you'll be better off loading up with tomato juice."

"Only if it has a smidgeon of vodka in it," squeaked Anne. "Listen, Jim. I don't know if OT was smart to hook up with Mercer on this project. Interpol is looking at his companies for all kinds of shady stuff, including cutting corners on contracts. Nothing ever gets proven, and witnesses have a way of disappearing."

"Unfortunately, we can't always know where Mercer gets his money," said Jim. "Fortunately, he's willing to take risks on projects, which could result in a lot of good. We can't tell OT to quit if we only have vague suspicions."

"This is always the dilemma if you're dealing with the devil," Anne said. "But like the devil, he's very smart. I don't know if I'm up to the job of handling this guy."

"I wouldn't worry too much about it, Anne," Jim said. "After all, you are in bed with Interpol. How could we go wrong?"

With that, Jim received a swift poke in the ribs"

The drone arrived on time, and the driver punched in the coordinates, sat back, and sipped his tea.

The bright Libyan sky was cloudless as the drone descended on the yacht's helipad in a cloud of scattering gulls. Con Mercer and his bikini-clad wife, Frances, expansive and smiling, greeted the two visitors from Ocean Technology, shepherding them adroitly to the *Fancy Fran's* saloon off the sky lounge.

Anne and Jim, suitably impressed, were offered a breakfast menu emblazoned with the FF logo. Mimosas and prawn canapés were served, and initial introductions were expanded to include some personal details on everyone present. Off in the distance, out in the Mediterranean, Doug Henson could be seen in one of the yacht's tenders, shooting at target buoys with what must have been an HCL pistol. Blue flashes could be seen and puffs of smoke as buoys were hit.

Distracted from the small talk, Jim interrupted Con to ask him if HCLs were legal in Libya. Mercer said he had a special license and was very proud of the government of Libya, which he said had been very accommodating to him and his companies.

"I am first and foremost a citizen of Libya, though I have several passports and speak three languages. Libya is the place I call home."

"You seem to be quintessentially European," Jim said.

"I was an immigrant to Libya from Germany, and I watched this country develop from a desert scrub to a vibrant democratic republic," Con continued. "Europe was the place I watched across the Mediterranean, and I was amazed at how long it took them to grow the European Union into the Republic of Europe, with fits and starts along the way. There were those who thought Europe would not survive the immigrant onslaught."

"I have to admit, Mr. Mercer, that I was one," said Jim. "In fact, I thought the chances for correcting climate change were better."

"Hindsight is always crystal clear, Dr. Foley," said Mercer. "But there was plenty of reason for cynicism years ago. From the outside one could only see a collection of enclaves in Europe. There were the Walloons, Flemish, Andalusians, Castilians, Valencians, Balearics, Galicians, Pomaks, Albanians, Macedonians, and on and on and on. Groups had their own religions, languages, cultures perpetuated for hundreds of years. There was no melting pot, as they say in the US, and outsiders couldn't merge if their lives depended on it, which they did. When you're too busy belly button-gazing, you can't see what's going on. Six hundred million people in hundreds of groups pulling in different directions."

"No group that large can ever be truly united without agreement on some common principles," Anne said.

"That's not enough," chimed in Jim. "The words in a charter or constitution or code have to be felt to the core, not just exist on the yellowing pages of history texts. That's why I think the combining of all the national armies into a common defense force, a common brotherhood, finally did the trick. They don't have to fight and die together, though that certainly unites folks. They only have to train together, live together, be together, inhale one another's humanity."

"You assume," said Mercer, "that the EDF is going to cement the union. Good luck with that. This is a work in progress."

Henson returned on the tender and eventually joined the group, saying, "The motorcade is available to travel to the first site as soon as you're ready, Mr. Mercer."

Jim noticed that Henson had the HCL strapped to his waist.

"Do you think you'll need that?" said Jim, pointing to the sidearm.

"There could be some bandits where we're going. Just a precaution," said Henson.

The trip to the motorcade site was short, but both Jim and Anne were growing increasingly apprehensive. Henson's presence and assurances didn't help matters.

After traveling several hours, they arrived at the first desert site in two large vans. A table, chairs, and shade canopy were set up. As Anne suspected earlier, she wouldn't have to do much walking. Jim, however, walked the length of the site, checking the terrain and taking samples of the sand.

"How about the lab setup?" Jim asked Henson.

"About a kilometer from here there is an old Italian monastery which has facilities and a large water cistern. The equipment you requested is in the van. After you check it out, we'll deliver it to the monastery and set it up for you."

Henson waved to three men who came with the party in the second van.

Lunch was arranged on the table, and Mercer, Jim, and Anne sat to dine and discuss the planned operation.

Jim began, "We'll fly the plant materials in from Benghazi. After we seed the selected sites with the 682B algae, we'll drop the aquabuds by drone at measured intervals."

"Aquabuds?" said Mercer. "What are aquabuds?"

Jim continued, "Aha! These are the key to the whole project: small plants, genetically related to cacti, but with very unique properties. They soak up and hold water for long periods. When placed on the sand, they will put long tendrils down, at the end of which pods will develop. When the temperature rises during the day, the stored water will be passed down to the pods to be stored below ground at lower temperatures. During the night, the water will return to the surface to be shared with the algae."

"How about the continuing water supply?" Mercer said.

"This section of the Libyan desert gets about one inch of rainfall a year. For each of our sites, that would be approximately eight million gallons. Ordinarily, this water would evaporate very quickly, but with the aquabuds, most will be retained," Jim said. "If we don't get this amount, we'll have to supplement from aquifers, but drilling will be risky and expensive."

"We can't guarantee success of the project because we can't guarantee the water supply," Anne said. "Our contract will provide for three months of algae growth. After which, we turn the sites over to Mercer Enterprises."

"What happens if I need additional water, but it's not ready?" Mercer said.

"The algae and aquabuds will not die. They'll go into a dormant state," Jim said.

Mercer frowned but seemed to be satisfied with Jim's response.

"After we seed, we'll have a technician here for the three months to oversee the project and take measurements," Jim said.

"No," blurted Mercer. "I don't want any technician. I want you, Dr. Foley. You're going to be the one bringing this project home. Just tell me what you need."

"That wasn't the arrangement, Mr. Mercer," said Anne.

"It is now. This is an e-mail from your CEO, Carl Schaefer, which guarantees your services until initial bloom at all sites and sequestration of carbon at specified three-month levels for 682B." Mercer waved the paper in Anne's face. "Now get to work, Ms. Baker, and draft the contract for my signature."

Anne certified the address and encryption then turned to Jim with knitted eyebrows, saying, "I'm sorry, Jim. I wasn't told of this."

Jim didn't like the sound of what he was hearing but had to marvel at Mercer's Machiavellian negotiation skills.

CHAPTER 19

Henson had business back in Kinsale and flew out of Benghazi the same night he left the desert site. The cargo compartment in his private plane contained a shipment of lyminiol disguised as coffee packs.

He read earlier in the *Journal* that two teenagers were found dead in Cork, poisoned by bad drugs probably bought in Kinsale. He also knew Enda McDonough's supplies were low and that he probably was cutting them with crap to keep his sales up. Enda didn't normally do this; though a lot of the greedy bastards that push the stuff wouldn't think twice about it. But if he was pressured by the need for funds and/or his addicted clientele, he wouldn't be immune from temptation. He pictured Enda going to the kids' funerals and commiserating with the grieving parents. *Such an asshole*, he thought.

When Jim Foley was told he would be staying in the Libyan desert for three months, he tried to call Caitlin on his mobile. He soon discovered he couldn't get service where he was. Henson offered to contact Jim's father to let him know of his predicament. Jim agreed but didn't mention Caitlin. He didn't want Henson calling or going anywhere near Caitlin. Telling his father would be good enough; she'd get the word.

Henson got a room in a B and B in Scilly and met with Savo and his two goons the following evening in the pub attached to the B and B. Henson and Savo had a love-hate relationship going back many years. Savo was one of the few people who could call Henson Meatface without suffering physical retribution. Henson needed Savo for the occasional difficult job, as he did for the hit on the Gardai drone.

"Anything I need to know about?" Henson asked Savo.

"We traded shots with the coast guard, Meaty, but we got away clean. Aside from Benny losing a piece of his finger, we hit 'em good. They backed off—probably called for reinforcements, but we was long gone in seconds," Savo said.

"Christ, Savo. That finger is DNA identification. Did you get it?" Henson asked.

"They won't get anything. It was burned to a frazzle. Benny will have to get something else to pick his nose, but otherwise, no loss."

Savo swigged his Guinness and pointed to the bandaged hand of his accomplice, laughing.

"I may have another job for you soon," Henson said. "I need to make a delivery to Enda McDonough if his new crypt is ready. I'll let you know in a day. Stay in the area."

"What's this? Did Enda tire of goin' to funerals, and he's now going straight to the graveyard?"

Savo paid the bill, and they all left amid more laughs.

Henson arranged to meet Enda up at the marina. When he arrived, Enda was standing beside some fishermen who were cleaning fish for tourists, patiently waiting with coolers. Several gulls were standing by on guano pancakes, hoping for some handouts. Enda was glad to see Henson when he called him aside.

"How is your mother, Enda?"

"Oh, she's up at Kinsale Hospital now, having a procedure. She's okay, though."

Enda didn't elaborate, and Henson didn't ask. Henson wanted to put Enda at ease so he could get some honest answers.

"Sorry about not getting any new supplies to you before sailing out of town," Henson said. "We had no choice. How have you been making out? Were you able to stretch things any?"

"The stuff I get from you is pretty high quality. At most, I add a bit of boric acid and lidocaine. I'm known for selling good stuff, and I like to keep it that way. I can't vouch for some of the dealers on my customer list."

Enda was aware of the recent teen deaths in Cork but tried to assure Henson that he wasn't responsible.

"Doesn't matter who did what, Enda. If they trace the stuff back to you, they'll eventually trace it to me and Mercer. I don't want them to get to you, and I damn sure don't want them to get to me." Henson drew his finger across his throat and then pointed at Enda. "If you have a dealer who's screwing with the product, let me know, and I'll have Savo pay him a visit."

Henson asked Enda how the crypt was coming along. He wanted to know when he could take delivery of more product.

"There's just some finishing touches left. I had to put in the family crest, make it look authentic. I think we could move stuff in now, keep it covered. No one will know," Enda said.

"That brings up another issue, Enda. The contractor is not one of us. How much does he know?"

Henson could see that Enda was getting uncomfortable.

"The contractor is a local guy. He maintains grave sites, landscapes, builds memorials and such. He knows nothing about our operations."

Enda remembered that he did tell Brenda Carter, the RTE reporter about his new crypt, but he would not mention this to Henson. He decided he should call this reporter and tell her that he was donating his crypt to St. Mary's, and this was her last chance to come see it. He really believed the young woman was interested in seeing his crypt.

"We have no one by that name," the voice at RTE said, and at that, Enda slowly came to the realization that he had been played.

In a very upset frame of mind, he called Henson and told him about Brenda.

"What did this Brenda look like?" Henson asked.

He suspected at once that she was the one and the same Brenda Delaney, the *Fancy Fran* ex-hostess who was probably a Gardai agent. He wondered where she was now. She was still a threat, unfinished business.

He thought of Savo, who said there were two cops in the Gardai drone they shot down. Henson checked the *Journal* report, which said that two Gardai officers were rescued and taken to hospital. There were no photos, but it mentioned that one was a female.

What were the chances this female cop was Brenda? he wondered. If a cop was heading out to a hundred-meter yacht to inspect for drugs, wouldn't he want the person with him to know exactly where to look? Yes, he was fairly certain that the female cop in the drone was Brenda.

Henson called Kinsale Hospital.

"I have a floral delivery for a police officer named Brenda, and I can't make out the last name. The chap that ordered it paid cash and signed the card, 'Your one and only.' Can you help me?"

"Let me check," the hospital person said, followed by a pause. "Oh yes. That was Garda Brenda Flaherty. She was transferred to St. James's Hospital in Dublin. Sorry."

Savo was tracing the posterior of a prostitute with practiced fingers when his mobile rang.

"I'll send Benny up to St. James's for a little slicing, Meaty. He only needs one good hand."

Henson thought even if it was the wrong Brenda, it was no loss. That's one less cop to piss him off.

Garda Brannigan and Garda Daly took some time off to visit Brenda in Dublin. They spent most of the day on a train, then got a lift to the hospital with a fellow Garda. Brenda was very popular with the Gardai in Dublin and had also been visited by concerned Special Forces guys from her old unit.

The St. James's was a premier facility in Ireland for the treatment of burns. Brenda received a skin graft on her damaged arm, and the surgery was excellent. She had much more healing to do and was being monitored closely for possible infection and other difficulties.

Daly left to get a cup of tea and told Brannigan he would meet him in the lobby. Brannigan continued to visit with Brenda but noticed that she was growing tired. He decided to leave when she nodded off, and he thanked a nurse on his way out.

When Brannigan reached the corridor, he saw a slightly hunched Benny walking in his direction, clutching wrapped flowers in one bandaged hand while his other hand remained inside his upper jacket. He didn't take much notice, smiled at the gent, who didn't smile back, but then saw something which he considered strange.

The guy was wearing dirty athletic shoes, something no policeman or ranger would wear on a hospital visit.

"Excuse me," Brannigan said, holding up his hand.

Benny threw the flowers at Brannigan and bolted down the corridor toward the exit, pulling a knife from his jacket as he sped. A large Special Forces troop coming in the opposite direction put his foot out to stop Benny, who tripped and went sprawling through an open door, across a balcony, over the railing, and to the street below. Benny cracked his head open and died instantly. He would no longer have to worry about his missing finger.

Chapter 20

Sabo called Henson with the bad news.

"I'm going to miss Benny. He'll be tough to replace, Meaty, a crack shot he was."

"Maybe so," said Henson, "but not so good with a knife."

"They're going to identify him and tie him to us. Get ready to be brought in and questioned. Shit, Meaty, that was a dumb move on our part. We should have known she would have been surrounded by cops," Sabo said.

"I hate to admit it, Sabo, but you're right. We can't use the crypt for drug storage anytime soon, maybe never. Scout up something else real fast in Cork if you have to. I'll tell Enda to lay low. And you be careful too. They're going to be watching you now."

Henson was steamed that Garda Brenda Flaherty slipped his heavy-handed retribution once again. He would have to let it go for now and hoped that nothing would get back to Mercer. He had other business to attend to.

Bob Foley missed Declan's company; though he knew Dec was better off doing light duty up in Dublin for the moment. He was also curious about why he had not heard from his son, Jim, for a while and decided to call Caitlin McGuinness to see if she could shed some light on the matter.

"Jim flew to Tripoli to meet Mercer, but I haven't heard from him in over a week. I thought he would be back by now, or at least call me and let me know what's going on," Caitlin said. "His company, Ocean Technology, told me he could be in Libya for a few months but couldn't give me any details."

Bob was now even more disturbed and called Mercer Enterprises. The woman answering Bob's call said she didn't know a Dr. Jim Foley but would check with Mr. Mercer's secretary. She took his name and number, but Bob felt in his gut that he would never hear from them. Bob then dredged up one of Jim's business cards and called the CEO of OT, Carl Schaefer. He thought he would get further than Caitlin since he would identify himself as Jim's father.

Carl Schaefer was actually glad to hear from Bob.

"I was just going to call you, Mr. Foley," he said. "As Jim's only living relative, I thought you must have heard from him recently. We agreed with Conrad Mercer that Jim would personally monitor his project through to completion, but we expected to get weekly progress reports. So far, we've heard nothing."

"Well, what does Mercer say?" Bob was getting increasingly irritated.

"Jim is working at sites in the Libyan desert, and Mercer says there is no cell phone coverage. Jim is being housed in an old monastery, which does have radio communication, but he hasn't heard from them either."

Schaefer said Mercer promised to send someone out by drone to check up, but that was two weeks ago. He then promised to let Bob know as soon as he heard something. Finally, Schaefer tried to assuage Bob by telling him that it was a very lucrative contract, and Jim should make out handsomely.

Bob called Caitlin to pass along what he was told. He told her not to worry, that Jim had been in worse spots—like avoiding a hurricane in the coral reefs. Caitlin said her father, Declan, was coming over and would call him later in the week.

Bob decided to pay another visit to the Dungeon, get one of their great meals, and think about his next meeting with Sarah Benjamin. He regretted that he had not kept in closer touch with her.

Doug Henson's brooding, scarred face was accented by silver-edged black clouds as he entered the Dungeon. Thanks to climate change, the temperature had reached twenty-five degrees Celsius, practically bikini weather for the Irish. There was a warm rain falling outside, and no doubt some of the locals would be complaining of a heat wave.

Legs with the pallor of alabaster could be seen padding around the dining room, and small talk about the weather was in abundance at the dark, dimly lit tables. Bob Foley had ordered a steak and was nursing a Jameson and soda when Henson slipped in beside him.

"Excuse this intrusion, Mr. Foley. I'm Doug Henson, security chief for Conrad Mercer."

"Yeah, I think I saw you once before in here when I was with Inspector McGuinness of the Gardai. I don't think he had very kind words for you. What do you want?"

Bob Foley thought in that instant that his pleasant evening was spoiled.

"I have news of your son, Dr. Jim Foley," Henson said. "He wanted you to know that he will be in Libya on his assignment per-haps three months—much longer than he originally thought. He is staying at an old Italian monastery, but he can't make or receive calls."

"I know that, Henson," said Bob. "But his boss at OT said Mercer was sending in a drone to check on his safety."

"I shouldn't be talking out of turn, Mr. Foley, but I don't think it was wise to have your son remain at that site. There are bandits in the area who could cause trouble." Henson beckoned to a waitress in a vampire cape with a tight bodice and ample cleavage. "Bring me what he has, and bring him another."

"Wait a minute," said Bob. "Why are you telling me this? Are you saying you actually give a damn about my son?"

"I want you to look at this photograph, Mr. Foley. Take your time." Henson took a small photo from his shirt pocket and handed it to Bob. The photo was old and faded but clear enough to distin-guish the features of a sixteen or seventeen-year-old boy with a slight grin, sitting at a table with an oriental couple. "That's the only photo I have of me and my foster parents. They died a year later in a plane crash, so it's the last photo taken of them."

Bob studied the photo carefully and realized that the boy resembled him to a startling degree, or at least the boy he was at age seventeen.

"What are you claiming, Henson—that we're related? I highly doubt that if that's what you're thinking."

"I didn't know my birth parents, and you didn't know yours. I've made some inquiries, and I know your foster father, JJ Foley left no record of your birth parents," said Henson.

"That's where your wrong, Henson," said Bob. "JJ left me a photo of my birth father, but it's not going to help you much. It's a fuzzy picture of a man with a full beard."

"You must give me a copy of that picture," said Henson. "I will give you a copy of mine."

Henson extracted another copy of his photo and handed it to Bob, who took it somewhat reluctantly.

"I will give you a copy of that picture," Bob said, "after you do something for me. I want you to get my son out of the desert safely, in one piece. I don't trust you, but I trust Mercer even less." Bob paused, then added, "You know, if you want to find out whether or not we're womb mates, DNA is the way to go. Give me a sample of your DNA and my friend, Declan McGuinness, can have a comparison run in no time. It would settle the question once and for all."

"Forget it," said Henson. "The only way McGuinness is getting my DNA is off my dead body." The busty vampire had returned with Bob's steak and salad and whisked away the empty glasses. "When I was first arrested years ago, I was routinely fingerprinted. Nowadays they do your DNA too, but not then. Privacy be damned."

"Tell you what," said Bob. "Since you're so interested in this crap, I'll give you the picture of my birth father and a copy of my DNA. Then you can play with it to your heart's content. Just get my son, Jim, out of Libya."

Henson left without saying a word after throwing a twenty euro note on the table. Bob leaned back, puzzled. Could it be possible he was related to this guy? *No, this was too big a stretch*, he thought. He decided to call Declan McGuinness but had to leave a voice mail. Declan would need to know about this curious interest of Henson in his genealogy.

He then called Sarah, wishing she was sitting across the table, sharing his ridiculous dilemma about Henson rescuing Jim. Sarah's call also went to voice mail, and he went back to musing about watching her beautiful, dark eyes twinkling in the faint glow from the candle on his table and haloed by her graying hair. She was touring with some art education group, and he wished she were with him now.

Bob's mobile rang. It was Declan returning his call. He was in Cork, having dinner with Caitlin, but said he would be back in Kinsale in the morning. Bob told him about his meeting with Henson, and Declan said he did have Henson's DNA, thanks to Garda Brenda Flaherty, who, incidentally, was healing very well. Since Bob was in the US Navy, his DNA was also readily available.

"Don't worry, Bob" Declan said. "I'll soon give you the good— or bad—news."

They both laughed, but the apprehension was evident.

CHAPTER 21

Jim Foley had two Libyan technicians that helped him with sequestration measurements, record-keeping, and other matters. They were soft-spoken, intelligent men, not connected to Mercer Enterprises or the goons that worked for Mercer, running operations at the monastery. He liked them, even developing a close bond with one, Sadiq.

Sadiq was in many ways like much of the workforce that cycled through Mercer's Libyan sites. The great majority were men from various locales in Asia, Africa, and India, with lined and worn faces in all shades of black, brown, yellow, and white; mostly young men separated from wives and families, eager to stay employed and earn enough to have something to send back home.

Sadiq was sent out to work at two of the sites, investigating an infestation of beetles that found the aquabs an irresistible source of water. This was causing destruction of the algae in the process. Sadiq had not returned after one visit, and hours passed with no communication.

Security was a continuing concern in the Libyan desert, and Mercer's operations were no exception. Against the objections of Henson, Mercer hired an insufficient number of guards to circulate and monitor activities. It didn't help matters that Henson was out of pocket back in Europe. Without his strong-arm oversight, the goons took advantage, preferring to lounge in camp, scarcely following a strict watch schedule.

Jim managed to persuade a search party to drive them out to the sites with two reluctant, armed guards. When the party arrived at Sadiq's campsite, they found it in disarray. Sadiq was found some distance away, badly beaten and wounded by laser burns. He managed to escape with his partner, who later died of his laser wounds alongside Sadiq. All Jim's equipment was stolen, but with the exception of Sadiq's eyewitness status, there would be no clue to the identity of the bandits.

The monastery went into lockdown, and frantic radio messages were sent to Mercer. Word came back from the Libyan authorities that the bandit, Abu Aldhiyb, a.k.a. Wolf, was seen in the area of the monastery, and precautions should be observed. It wasn't clear what that meant since the Libyan militia was located hours away from the site, and good radio and mobile communication was now a thing of the past.

Jim was quite saddened by the attack on Sadiq and the death of his partner. Colleagues were organizing a small memorial service and trying their best to contact relatives in Benghazi. Sadiq's account of the attack seemed to confirm that Wolf was indeed the culprit.

Jim was inexperienced in the use of small arms but thought it best that he should gain some familiarity with the use of the HCL in the event the worst-case scenario came to pass. Mercer's goons no longer feared that Jim would attempt to leave and offered to provide him a weapon and a primer on its use. The monastery was now prepared for an onslaught, but the crew made one fatal mistake.

The monastery was supplied water from a large cistern located fifty meters from the main dwelling. The cistern was, in turn, supplied by a ground well that was sunk over four hundred meters to one of the few aquifers in southern Libya. This water was, in fact, the supply that was used to initially charge the algae fields and aquabuds. The size of the aquifer wasn't known as it was tapped in the forties and not used a great deal since.

The monastery crew left one man to secure the cistern and became complacent when nothing happened after a week. After two weeks, the cistern supply was shut down, and all contact was lost with the security guard. Another man was sent to the cistern at night, and he, in turn, disappeared; the cistern remained offline.

There were six persons remaining in the monastery, all well-armed but totally dependent on a limited water supply coming from two small tanks in the building. All Wolf had to do was wait them out. They would have to surrender to avoid dying of thirst. The bandits flaunted their superior position by turning on a light at the well shack by the cistern and playing music, which drifted out on the desert air.

The head of the crew suggested that they find out what the bandits wanted and try to negotiate their release. This idea was abandoned when no one would volunteer to approach the bandits with a white flag.

It was then suggested they could take the truck and rush the well shack, taking a chance that their HCL blasts would not damage the water supply. They soon discovered that the truck had been disabled. The guy who had been sent to retake the water supply was their only mechanic.

Eventually, water became severely rationed, and Jim suggested he take a few of the technicians out to the algae fields at night and dig up a cart load of aquabuds. This would keep them going a bit longer. Hopefully, by then a rescue party would get to them. Mercer had to know there was trouble when the reports stopped coming. In fact, a drone was probably already in the air.

Armed with HCLs and canisters of some of the last of their precious water, Jim and two technicians set out in the cold night air on a long trek to the algae fields. The remaining crew fired diversionary HCL blasts at the well shack, calibrated to annoy the bandits but not destroy the building or equipment.

The ruse was successful, but the mission was far from over and full of peril. The trek was exhausting, and the exertions prompted bodily demands for even more fluids, making the thirst excruciating. One of the technicians offered Jim half his water ration on the assumption that, as a native, he was better able to withstand the rigors than Jim. Jim refused his offer but found it difficult to talk with his swollen tongue. He just waved him off.

When they reached the first algae field, they fell on the ground, clawing at the sand, ripping at the algae to pull up the buried aquabuds. The squeezed-out water filled their mouths and ran down their faces, a small but blessed relief.

The three stood to survey the field ahead. The ground lit by a bright moon became suddenly brighter and bluer with flashes from behind. The sound of HCLs broke the silence, and the two technicians accompanying Jim fell over with holes burned through the back of their chests. The agony of realization burned in Jim's eyes as a voice from behind told him to drop his weapon. Ahead and to the east, a pair of headlights flicked on, and a barely discernible vehicle, painted desert sand, came more clearly into view in a cloud of fine sand—a hovercraft.

"Dr. Foley, don't worry about your friends at the monastery. You will not be seeing them again."

Wolf sat in the back of the sand-colored vehicle while Jim was pushed, hands tied into the front. Wolf was wearing a white turban and loose clothing, spoke good English with a London public-school accent. His face was dark and narrow, sporting a well-manicured Van Dyke. He waved his hand, and the vehicle sped into the night, suspended over the sand. The "driver" had little to do but check a radar screen.

They arrived sometime later at the base of a large rock outcrop. A long, narrow tent with walls of translucent plastic was spread out in front of them, lighted dimly from the inside. A low stone building with barred windows and a heavy door nestled in the sand between the tent and the outcrop, obviously some type of prison. Jim was escorted to this building, where he was locked inside after his hands were untied. He was told to eat, drink, and rest; Wolf would see him in the morning.

Inside this jail, Jim could see he had a table, chair, cot, and adjacent privy, all primitive. He had a small stumpy candle for light and a box of matches. A jug of water and plate of some kind of stew had been placed on the table. The water was lukewarm and the stew cold. Of course, he didn't know what was in the stew and decided not to eat it. He drank the water ravenously, however, deciding it had a slight flavor of something he didn't want to think about. The aquabud squeezings actually tasted better, but his swollen tongue was grateful for any kind of moisture.

Jim slept fitfully, mourning the loss of his technicians and vowing that, somehow, they would be avenged. He wished Sadiq was with him but feared that everyone at the base camp must be dead or scattered if Wolf was to be believed. He could not imagine why Wolf had not killed him too. His half-conscious thoughts wandered to Caitlin, his beautiful Caitlin. He feared that he would never see her again and tried to picture what their children would have looked like—a potential future now lost in the sands of Libya.

Jim was awakened at daybreak when a pail of water was thrown in his face, precious water which spilled across his salty skin. It felt and tasted wonderful, and ironically, he smiled at his jailor. When he exited the privy, his hands were again tied, and he was led outside until the sun was fully risen. The glaring heat subsided only when he entered Wolf's tent and crossed to a table spread with fruit and yogurt.

"We live simply out here, Dr. Foley, but you are a special guest. Enjoy our meager hospitality while you can." Wolf was seated cross-legged, sipping tea. There were two other swarthy men off to the side in the large tent. "When we saw the equipment your helper had and checked his notes, we knew that someone special was working at the old Italian monastery. Dr. James Foley of Ocean Technology. What would OT and Mercer Enterprises pay to get you back, Dr. Foley?"

"I think you would be disappointed." Jim's swollen tongue still made speaking difficult.

"Oh no, Doctor. Don't underestimate your worth," said Wolf. "I checked, and you have six patents in your name. I think you are worth at least ten million euros to the deep pockets that put you out here." One of the men stepped forward, raised a mobile phone, and took several photos of Jim. "We can't make calls from out here, but we can take pictures. Wonderful gadgets. We also found some very private e-mail addresses in the notes. When we get to a terminal, I'm sure those on the other side will be happy to know you are safe and sound—and what it will take to keep you that way."

CHAPTER 22

Deb Benjamin was very unique in her approach to landscape design. Certainly, she had a prodigious knowledge of plants of all kinds, together with the biological backdrop required for the staging of living things in a fluid design. She knew how to use line, form, color, construction, and seasonal change in her creations. More than that, however, she felt it necessary to research the history of the place, which formed the palette for her art. For her, a landscape would have to breathe a history, provoke past and future emotions, and evoke memories. To her, any location where humans once held sway or presently tread had a story to tell, one which could somehow be blended into her total landscape package. Her clients often had other ideas, but Deb was very good at convincing them to see and agree to the lasting beauty in her vision.

So it was that Deb was eager to accept the challenge of Sham Rock. She arranged to meet with Bob and explore the site, ask questions, and take notes. She was aware that her sister, Sarah, and Bob had a childhood history and that JJ Foley was a mentor as well as a father to Bob and an influence on Sarah. She would have to find out more about Otis Sham and find out if he had any connection with JJ. She wondered how JJ came to buy the property and what attracted him to it.

News files from the time before and during JJ's purchase did reveal some interesting things about Otis Sham. It seems he was frequently a person of interest with the Gardai for local smuggling activities and suspicious financial dealings. He had no known relatives and died intestate, leaving many debts and unpaid taxes. The Rock was sold at auction by the county, and JJ was able to acquire the property for a price well below the assessed valuation. So JJ never knew Sham and only learned of his reputation much later.

As frequently happens with persons who develop a reputation and then disappear from public view, memory erodes the hard spots and builds legends to fill the gaps. So it is that Otis Sham was mythologized and even in some quarters eulogized. Some even said that there was a body buried up in Sham Rock. When Scarlet Kelly was found on the Scilly beach, more than a few dredged up the old legend.

Deb was mentally filing these thoughts when she met with Bob Foley and began her tour of the property. Donal Riordan offered to show Deb around when Bob was suddenly called away by the contractor, Stitch Hegarty. The day was warm and sunny, so Donal was in a rare good mood.

"I think a lot of these feckin' trees should be cut down myself."

"A few, maybe," Deb said. "Most of them will do fine with a good pruning by a qualified arborist. We want to avoid butchery."

"Who's the 'we,'" said Donal. "I'm the only one that cuts the damned things. I go by what's dead and what's living."

"Of course," Deb said, smiling broadly. "We'll get them shaped right, and then you can keep them that way." She then realized the implications of what she said, and her smile quickly faded. "Actually, once they're pruned properly, they will require little care for a long time."

They emerged on the most overgrown section of the property, and Deb was making notations furiously.

"Do you not get back here often, Donal?"

"Aye," said Donal. "This is one of the feckin' places that requires little care over a long time."

He smiled as an eye and a tooth glinted in the sun. She pointed to a pile of bramble and asked him what was beneath.

Donal swept the bramble aside, and a large, rusty slab of metal was exposed. It was apparently painted dark green at one time but was scarred with years of weathering.

"Old Otis used this spot to dump his junk," said Donal. "Wasn't harming anything, and Bob didn't want me fussing with it."

Deb ran her fingers along the edge of the metal and then suddenly stopped.

"This feels like a hinge." She reached down to a lower spot. "Yes, three hinges in this thing."

Donal stepped in and brushed away layers of loose rust on the side opposite the hinges. He grasped at a bar rusted fast in two holes.

"By God, we may have found where Sham buried his bodies. Let me get a pry bar."

He returned in a few minutes and pounded on the bar until it jiggled loosely.

Eventually, with Deb helping him, Donal pried the metal door loose and raised it to reveal steps descending into pitch blackness.

"Why did I not know about this before," he blurted. "I have to get Bob Foley to see this."

Returning with two flashlights and Stitch Hegarty, Bob and Donal made their way down the steps and into a small room cut into the rock, damp but not dripping wet. The air smelled strongly of mold and decay. Bob instinctively put a handkerchief to his mouth and nostrils.

Observing this, Donal said, "I thought so. You're smelling Sham's bodies. The stories are true."

"I'm afraid not," Stitch said from the base of the steps, pointing to a dead rat on the floor. "It didn't take much of a hole for him to get in. I don't think he's been here too long, so he can't be one of Sham's bodies."

Bob played the light into the corner of the underground cell and spotted a large black metal safe. The dial on the safe was difficult to move at first but then yielded and clicked as it turned.

"All I need now is the combination," said Bob. "I don't think we'll get that anytime soon."

He then tried to move the safe, but it was rock solid.

"Well, let's see," said Deb. "There are the usual suspects. Did Otis Sham even know his birth date? He could have used that for the combination."

By this point, the four onlookers, though stunned by the finding, were realizing there was likely something valuable in the safe and curiosity peaked. Bob asked Stitch if he knew someone who could drill out the lock.

"There's a guy I know in Cork who could probably do it. I'll give him a call," Stitch said.

"The safe is big enough to contain a feckin' body. I'm not giving up on that yet." Donal was running his fingers around the edge of the door to see how well it was sealed. "A little explosive might be faster than drilling, Stitch."

"The usual suspects," Deb repeated. "Look at the back of the door we came in. Otis scratched some numbers there in the corner. Want to bet it's the combination?"

"You're a sweetheart, Plant Lady," said Donal. "If I wasn't such a lost cause, I'd ask you to marry me."

Bob spun the dial a few times then tried the first number going clockwise then counterclockwise for the second number and so on. Deb took some flash pictures with her mobile as the door seal popped, and Bob gently opened the safe door. The four jaws of the onlookers fell open. In the glow of the electric torch, stacks of gold coins glinted back at them.

"Jaysus! It's not a body, Donal, but I'll take it." Bob gasped. "I'll have to get these appraised, but I reckon there's a fortune here."

When Declan McGuinness arrived at the Rock, and Bob showed him what they found, he got Brannigan and Daley to accompany Bob as escorts. They transported the haul to a bank vault in Cork, where an appraiser estimated the value of the coins at 12.5 million euros.

"Don't get your hopes up too high, Bob. We'll have to check the provenance of this stuff. Otis was not known for dealing on the up and up. We could be looking at stolen goods."

"There's also another little thing called the 1987 National Monuments Act," said Declan. "Be thankful the coins weren't found using a metal detector. The unlicensed use of which is banned in Ireland and fined heavily. But even if you didn't use a detector, the coins could be confiscated. In this case, you would be paid a finder's fee, just a percentage of the actual value."

"You're shitting me, Declan," said Bob. "The appraiser said those coins were minted in Germany during the nineteen-forties. They were probably brought here to fund sabotage operations in WWII. They're not antiquities."

"Not antiquities, Bob, but they have historical value. I think the National Museum might be interested. You'll have to wait on their final judgement," said Declan.

"The RTE wants to interview me about the find," said Bob. "I don't know how they got word, but this is a small town, and this is a big item. I may be able to get the public on my side once they know about a possible confiscation."

"Don't count on it, Bob," Said Declan. "It's amazing how many of your neighbors can become sore losers when reality sets in."

CHAPTER 23

The Mercer Enterprises Libyan site had only rudimentary medical facilities. The basic idea was that medical emergencies would be handled by flying the patient to Benghazi. As such, Sadiq's dressings and medication were expected to hold him until he could be flown out, but this, of course, would not be happening. Most of the crew at the site were killed by Wolf's men, but Sadiq and a few of the custodial personnel were able to commandeer a vehicle and drive into the desert before Wolf launched his attack. They drove to a large outcropping and covered the vehicle with a tarp to disguise it.

Sadiq knew that Jim was taken prisoner and suspected that Wolf might be looking for ransom. He decided to leave the others after some hesitation. He figured he would probably die of infection if he didn't get back to Benghazi and so had little choice; also, he hoped he might be able to locate Jim Foley, and they could escape together. He would need Jim as much as Jim needed him. He assumed that Jim would be at Wolf's camp, so this was a further downside.

Sadiq and his group waited until they saw no signs of activity back at the site and then motored slowly at night to the main compound. After scouring the area and poking through smoking ruins, Sadiq found what he was looking for. One of the drones had been hangared for minor repairs but was left intact. It was a small drone but could be charged from the storage cell near the water cistern and flown at least some of the distance to Benghazi.

Sadiq's first problem, not considering his failing physical condition, was to find out where Wolf's camp was located. He convinced his colleagues to search the dead bodies of the bandits to see if they could find a clue.

"This one has some kind of a map!" a dark man shouted after an hour of searching. He held up a square of dirty, folded paper, wrinkled and bloodstained.

Sadiq spread the map out on the ground and recognized some familiar features. Mercer's site was indicated by a scratched "X," and a penciled notation near it read "209." He thought the man with the map must have been a driver who would need directions from Wolf's camp.

Sadiq's bloody bandage was itching and probably needed to be changed. He ignored the feelings of discomfort so that he could concentrate on the meaning of the notation. If he was at Wolf's camp and needed directions to Mercer's site, he would only need two things: bearing and distance. In the desert, with no roads and a paucity of markers, the compass took the place of road signs. Three numbers were okay for a bearing but didn't supply a distance. He puzzled about this briefly because he decided he had to find the dispensary and get his bandage changed before he passed out.

One of the men went with him to the small dispensary, which was a room in the main compound. The room was trashed, but they were able to find salve and bandages in sufficient quantity to dress Sadiq's wounds. One of the wounds looked particularly nasty, and unfortunately, there was no antiseptic in the salve. Sadiq found some bleach and rubbed it on the infected tissue. He winced in excruciating pain, which brought tears to his eyes. Eventually, his mind struggled back to the problem of escape.

Sadiq decided to accept the "209" as a bearing. This would mean that the direction to Wolf's camp from Mercer's site would be twenty-nine degrees northeast (bearing 029), but how far he needed to travel on that bearing was still a puzzle.

In the desert, distance was frequently measured by how long your water supply would last or how far your fuel or electric charge would take you. Both things were existential concerns. Sadiq decided Wolf and his minions had cased Mercer's site and would want to travel light, not hauling extra tanks and cells. He would locate within safe hauling distance of a water source, sufficiently hidden from satellite pickup or drone surveillance. Putting all this together and checking the map again for the right features, Sadiq decided Wolf's camp was located 250 to 300 kilometers to the northeast.

He carefully checked over the drone and decided the required repairs were limited to body work and doors that didn't close properly. He was no mechanic, but it looked like the motors and electronics were functioning well enough to risk the journey. He then had a bad feeling in the pit of his stomach when he started the rotors. A high-pitched whine indicated that at least one set of bearings was faulty. He asked one of the other men to try his hand, and both decided the problem was limited to one motor. The remaining motors would automatically adjust and stabilize the craft if the bad motor shut down, that is, if the electronics were fully functional. Of course, the maneuverability and speed of the drone would be limited, but not by a critical amount. Still, flying would be risky.

Sadiq obtained some cotton from the dispensary and plugged his ears as best he could. He loaded a box of packaged food items, medical bandage, extra water, and two HCL pistols into the rear of the drone. He gritted his teeth, rubbed his sore wounds, and climbed onto the drone. He would be traveling alone but told the men remaining at the site that he would send help as soon as he was able to restore communication with Baghdad. He punched in the compass bearing, the Auto Pilot and the Start button. The rotors gained speed, but miraculously the volume of the whine from the bad motor reduced somewhat as the speed increased. He was grateful for this counterintuitive event but feared some other ill wind would blow his way—"Murphy's Law," Jim Foley would call it.

Sadiq put the air-conditioning on low to conserve the batteries; as a result, the heat inside the drone rose to thirty-five degrees Celsius. Sweat rolled down Sadiq's face, making vision difficult as he scanned the horizon for some sign of the scrubby features he thought would not be far from Wolf's camp. He was getting increasingly despondent, realizing that his entire venture was built on guesswork. The sun was setting, and he would have to put down and wait for morning. He had plenty of battery left but wasn't sure the motors would turn over after two hours of running hot, followed by the chill of the Libyan night. As the drone descended, he thought he saw a large rock outcrop, a column of smoke, and a small, flickering light in the distance. His spirits climbed instantly until he realized his predicament.

If the signs were correct, he had landed to within a kilometer of Wolf's camp. He would not be able to fly any closer for fear that the whine of the drone would give him away. In fact, he may have already been compromised. He didn't know how to disable the defective motor without risking the integrity of the electronics for the whole system. The blunt truth was clear: he would have to dismount and walk the rest of the way with a backpack of essential gear, hoping that he would not crumble from his injuries along the way. Also, Wolf's perimeter defenses would need to be penetrated with stealth, and Sadiq didn't think he was up to the task. This entire mission was a big gamble from the onset. He would not last a day in the heat of the sun, so his foot journey would have to be completed in the early hours or at night. He didn't know what to do, but for now, the drone cab was the best place to be. He could retire in relative safety and get something to eat.

Sadiq was not a man to wallow very long in a funk, despite his current physical condition. He eventually decided he was going about his situation the wrong way. Stealth was not the solution. He thought what he needed to do was fly the drone directly into the middle of the camp and create a diversion while he scampered to the nearest cover. He would disable the safety and let the power on one of his HCLs climb exponentially to the point that the pistol would explode, creating the sound and light show needed to mask his escape. The downside to this plan was removing himself and his kit from the conflagration fast enough to stay in one piece. This was very risky but, considering his options, seemed to be the best course.

Sadiq decided to engage his plan the following night. He had a difficult time falling asleep given his discomfort and angst and later that night was roused to fitful wakefulness by lights stabbing through the murky space of the cabin. He rubbed his eyes and thought he saw a hulking shape moving toward the drone. The cabin door was noisily yanked open.

"You must be Sadiq. Glad we found you in one piece," Henson said. "You need medical attention, but I can't help you with that now. Are you able to get about?"

"I can move, Mr. Henson," Sadiq said. "You are a welcome sight."

He knew of Henson's reputation for harshness, but his feeling of relief was genuine. Henson would be a good match for Wolf, and the prospect of getting to Baghdad was looking better.

"Do you know if Jim Foley is with Wolf?" Henson asked. "Have you seen him?"

Sadiq explained his situation and told Henson that he could only assume Jim Foley was being held in Wolf's camp. He went through his plan to get into the camp and try to rescue Foley and escape. Henson's scarred brow knitted, then he laughed.

"You are either very brave or a resurrection of Don Quixote," Henson said. "Your plan to crash the drone in the camp is good, but the first thing we need to do is find out what kind of defensive measures Wolf has deployed. He knows we will be coming, and I hope he doesn't know we're here already."

Henson's drone was parked behind some desert scrub, and the two men he brought with him were pulling a robot scout out of the cargo bay. It was a tracked vehicle with the capability of lifting over obstacles. Henson was staring at a dimly lighted screen on a control box he deftly juggled.

After the robots rumbled out of sight, he mumbled, mostly to himself, "Oh yeah! Five infrared (IF) scanners set up in a perimeter around his camp." He turned to Sadiq. "Anyone of them can pick up a warm body out to one hundred meters and then laser it on command."

"Can you disable them?" Sadiq asked.

He was wondering whether or not Henson would include him in the raid considering his infirmity. He soon had his answer.

"The instant our robot takes out the scanners, Wolf will know we're here," Henson said. "I want to send your drone into the center of the camp and explode it remotely. That distraction should give us a bit of a head start." Ominously he added, "We shouldn't need you to set up the drone."

CHAPTER 24

Bob Foley wanted to discuss his meeting with Henson at the Dungeon in Kinsale. He needed Declan's help and advice more than ever. Declan was convinced that Henson had killed Scarlet Kelly, so he probably wouldn't accept that there was any good intention in Henson's offer to get his son, Jim, out of Libya. Bob decided to bring it up at breakfast.

The following morning Declan was slathering orange marmalade on an English muffin when Bob poured his guest a cup of tea. Declan enjoyed being back at the Rock where he could follow the restful passage of the Bandon River and spend time with his old friend, Bob Foley. Unfortunately, now the Bandon brought back the additional memory of helplessly careening into the Atlantic in a shot-up drone, with Brenda Flaherty bleeding, unconscious next to him. He hated the ocean, which was the subject of more than a few of his nightmares.

"What's on your agenda today, Dec?" Bob asked.

"I'm bringing Enda McDonough in for questioning, Bob," said Declan. "I want to know what he knows about the attempted murder of Garda Brenda Flaherty in a Dublin hospital. What about you?"

"I'll probably be talking to Stitch about his work on the cellar passage and ask him to check out this new bunker in the yard. Also, I want to know if it's worth my while to haul that safe out of here. But, more important than all of that, I need to show you the picture Henson gave me in the Dungeon."

Bob saw Declan's eyebrows raise at the mention of Henson.

Declan said he didn't get a comparative analysis of Bob's and Henson's DNA but would do that today. He took the photo from Bob and studied it carefully.

"That's a remarkable resemblance to you when you were young. I knew you in your twenties, but one doesn't change that much from their late teens, I don't think. Tell you what. I'll have an age progression done on the photo and get back to you."

"What do you think about him getting Jim out of Libya?" Bob asked.

"Hell, that's his job as Mercer's security man. I wouldn't worry about it, Bob. Sounds like he might be all the more solicitous if he thinks Jim is a nephew. I think that was the whole point of his meeting with you. Doesn't matter though. One way or another, he's going down." With that, Declan grabbed his umbrella and headed out the door.

Declan wasn't gone fifteen minutes when Bob's mobile rang.

"Mr. Foley, this is Carl Schaefer with Ocean Tech. Conrad Mercer called me today with some bad news, and I thought I'd better let you know right away. His drone reached the site of their desert project last evening, and your son was not there. Several of the workers and technicians had been killed, and the site was trashed, but since Dr. Foley wasn't located, it appears he was taken hostage by a bandit called Wolf."

Bob turned pale and grabbed at his chest and said, "Is anyone looking…"

"The Libyan authorities sent out a search party. They think he may have been taken in some kind of aerial vehicle since they found no tracks—perhaps a drone or an air car," Schaefer said.

"Who can I talk to there?" Bob asked.

"Best thing to do is to call Doug Henson. He's Mercer's security officer, and he'll be landing in Benghazi tonight to take charge of the project and liaise with the Libyan militia. The Libyan officer-in-charge doesn't speak good English, but he and Henson have worked together before, or so Mercer tells me."

"Mercer is the reason this whole thing went down," said Bob, livid with rage. "He was the one who insisted that Jim stay at this godforsaken place for the entire duration of the project. A perfect target for ransom—an Irish American scientist. That desert rat bastard wouldn't have attacked the site if the only thing there were Libyan technicians and Mercer goons."

"I'm sorry, Mr. Foley. I was complicit in that decision. We will do all we can to get Jim out unharmed. The State Department and the FBI are working this with Interpol and Libya—" Schaefer was cut off.

"Great," said Bob. "This is just what we need to get maximum media attention. The kidnapper will love this. I just hope he doesn't have an ideological ax to grind, or Jim will wind up headless in the sand!" He was greeted by silence, and then he apologized to Schaefer. "I'm sorry, Mr. Schaefer. You couldn't have foreseen this outcome, and it's unfair…"

"From what I have heard of this kidnapper, he understands only one thing. When we get a ransom demand, we'll know where we stand," said Schaefer. "We will get Jim back. I won't pretend to understand what you must be going through, but you have communicated your pain loud and clear, and I take it to heart."

After Schaefer ended his call, Bob knew he would have to endure the added angst of calling Caitlin and filling her in before she heard it on the news. It turned out to be every bit as difficult as he imagined.

"How ironic," said Caitlin tearfully. "We're looking to the man my father has alleged is a murderer to save Jim."

Bob thought to himself that the most crushing irony would be Henson turning out to be "family."

Bob wanted to talk to Declan but resisted calling him. He didn't relish the idea of disrupting Declan's work day with his troubles. Declan would be staying in Kinsale at least another day, so he would see him in the evening. Besides, he wanted to be sure Declan had enough time to find out if he was truly related to Henson. He thought to send Declan a text reminder but resisted that also.

The notion of ransom generated a flood of thoughts in his head. It seemed fortuitous, providential, that Otis Sham's gold coins turned up as they did. There was increasing pressure now for the government to release the coins for his use. Declan could help with that. The pressure on Bob was overwhelming, and he decided to get out of the Rock and take Scilly Walk up to the pub. Stitch had not arrived yet, so he had plenty of time.

He arrived at the pub and ordered a ham-and-cheese sandwich and a Guinness ale. There was no one in the pub but a couple of tourists, probably from Scotland by the sound of them. His thoughts turned back to ransom, and he remembered the anecdotal and factual things he had been told over the years. First, even if a ransom is paid, odds are that the victim will be killed anyway. Second, if no ransom is requested, it probably means that the victim was killed—extra baggage. Third, these thoughts weren't helping at all.

He decided to take his drink and head outside to a table where he could watch the gulls wheeling overhead. There was one which landed nearby, hoping to cadge some tidbit or other. Bob obliged by throwing him a scrap of bread. At that moment, Bob's mobile rang.

"Bob, you're an old Navy guy," said Declan. "You'll understand it when I tell you, 'Stand by for a ram!' You have a twin brother!"

"You're sure," Bob gurgled.

"No doubt," Declan said. "DNA doesn't lie. 98 percent certainty. Also, I had Henson's photo age enhanced, and guess what? It's you! I always thought if I had a brother that I'd want him to be you. Now that son of a bitch beat me out. Never mind. I'm still going to take that killer down."

Bob Foley, retired Navy commander, leaned his head back and sobbed quietly. This was too much: a major gold find, the kidnapping of his only son, and now this. He wiped the tears from his mobile and returned it to his pocket without mentioning a word about Jim's kidnapping to Declan.

"Are you all right, laddie?" A white-topped pink face hovered over Bob.

"Oh, I just had some good news," Bob said.

"Then we should celebrate," the face said. "Let me buy you another Guinness. You have a strange reaction to good news, but who am I to argue?"

After a while, Bob left the pub and decided to head for the stone beach. He took his shoes off so that he could feel the impact of the jagged stones as he walked back toward the Rock. He didn't get far before the cuts and scrapes forced him to decide that he had enough painful reality for one day, and he climbed back to the paved path.

Stitch arrived at the Rock shortly before Bob reached the oak door, and the diversion was welcome.

CHAPTER 25

Declan seated Enda McDonough in a back room at the Kinsale Garda Station. There was no one-way mirror in the wall, but a small video camera in the corner with a flashing red light took everything in.

"This won't take long, Enda. There's just a few things to clear up, and I know you'll be happy to do that as you did before," Declan said.

"Before I got a sandwich and a brew at the pub. What am I going to get this time?" Enda shuffled his feet and chewed on a cinnamon stick.

"First, I should say that I'm sorry about your mother, but I'm sure it must be some relief for you," Declan said, changing the subject from food and drink. "Without your mother's welfare check coming in, though, I hope you're not finding it more difficult to make ends meet."

"If so, it wouldn't be much of a relief then, would it? Mom is better off, and I'm doing fine, Inspector," said Enda.

"What are you doing these days, Enda? Employment up at the marina can't be too steady." Declan shoved photos of three men under Enda's nose, two of them Sabo and Benny. "Did any of these guys approach you about a job?"

"I don't know them, never seen either," said Enda.

"That's not true, Enda. You were seen talking to these guys, and I know you talked to this girl too." Declan pushed another photo of Brenda Flaherty up to Enda.

"Yeah, I talked to her. She said she was a reporter, but she was a damn cop. She played me," Enda burbled.

"How did you know she was a cop, Enda?" asked Declan.

"Doug Henson told me she was a hostess on his yacht, so I knew she wasn't a reporter. She played us both."

Enda realized he said too much, but he couldn't walk it back.

Declan lied when he said Enda was seen talking to the three guys, but he knew they were known associates of Henson. Now he was sure Henson had ordered the hit on Brenda and was probably also behind the shooting down of the drone. Henson was on his way to Benghazi, and Sabo couldn't be located, but there would be more interrogations.

When Declan arrived back at the Rock that evening, he was worried about Bob's state of mind after he dropped the bomb about Henson being his brother. When he saw his old friend, however, it was clear something larger was occupying Bob's mind.

"Dec, Jim's been kidnapped in the Libyan desert, and Mercer is sending Henson to find him," blurted Bob.

He told Declan as much as he knew, and both men poured large whiskies and flopped into overstuffed chairs.

Declan stared straight ahead and said, "How the hell am I going to have Henson hauled in by Interpol for questioning when he's right now tracking Jim's kidnapper? He and Mercer know the lay of the land over there and are probably the best ones to find that bad guy."

"That's a scary thought, Dec," said Bob. "I'm thinking I need to get word to him that Jim is his nephew, and it might give him a heightened sense of urgency. What do you think?"

"Do it. Send him a text. I'll give you the contact information on the card he gave me on the yacht," said Declan. "This whole thing is a shit shake, Bob. I'm sorry you have to go through it. What a day for you."

"There's been no word on ransom," Bob said. "This has me worried. But who would this asshole contact? Mercer Enterprises? Ocean Technology? Me?"

"I'm betting it'll be the deepest pockets—Mercer," said Declan. "The FBI will be tapping Con Mercer's mobile and try to track the call with a satellite locator, but these days, there are a lot of different, safer means the kidnapper could use."

"I have a hunch he'll contact me," said Bob. "He may not know what funds I have, but he knows I'm in contact with those who have the money, and he knows I have the biggest reason for getting Jim back."

Bob and Declan retired early. Declan said he was going to Cork in the morning to see if the Gardai could get a line on Sabo and if anything turned up on the gold coins. He said he would call Bob later in the day to check on developments with Jim. The text had been sent to Henson, but there was no acknowledgement of receipt. The morning turned out to be cloudy, warm, and windy—a good cocktail for afternoon rains.

Just after noon the postman arrived, popped a letter in the mailbox at the oak door, rang the bell, and left. The letter had a Libyan stamp and postmark. A single folded sheet of paper with a typed message inside read:

> *Mr. Foley, you will transfer ten million euros to the following Swiss account by 1600 GMT, 30 Sept, or the next package you receive will contain some very familiar fingers.*

There was a string of numbers and letters at the bottom and a wolf logo. Bob put the letter and envelope in a plastic bag, took it in the house, and texted Carl Schaefer at OT. Within an hour, an American FBI special agent arrived at the Rock, introduced himself, left a card, and took the plastic bag from Bob.

"Good news," said Declan when he called that afternoon. "The Dublin Antiquities Council weighed in and said they have no legal claim to your gold coins. They were left on your property by the previous owner and have no archival value beyond their intrinsic worth. The Gardai could find no record of lost or stolen property meeting the description of these coins going back 150 years. This would predate the mintage year stamped on them. Nazi Germany might be able to claim them, but they're not about to step up. Beats me how Otis Sham got his paws on them."

"How interesting, Dec," said Bob. "I've come into a fortune, and I'll have to give most of it to a kidnapper as ransom for Jim." Bob described the letter he received, which the FBI traced to a post office in Benghazi. "They think Henson might have a lead on the kidnapper, but he's not sharing information. Also, Henson must have destroyed his mobile because they can't trace it. He doesn't want any 'interference' from law enforcement."

"What about Mercer Enterprises and Ocean Tech?" Declan asked. "Are they stepping up?"

"The policy for both companies is not to pay ransom, as this could jeopardize other employees and operations. Carl Schaefer at OT said they have a special fund they could go into, but since I have the gold coin assets, that's off the table." Bob said he would have to convert the gold to cash and hope the appraisers were on target about the value. "Even if the kidnapper doesn't get his hands on the money, he has to see that sufficient assets were transferred to his account by September 30, or he's liable to start cutting fingers."

"Let's hope the FBI is correct about Henson being closest to finding Jim," Declan said.

The afternoon rains finally came and succeeded in heightening the gloomy atmosphere around Sham Rock.

Declan met with Caitlin that evening at a restaurant in Cork. He wanted to take her to dinner and provide some fatherly support to his only daughter in this time of trial. He knew she would be imagining terrible outcomes for Jim and the loss of their future together. He really had no good news and hesitated to say that Jim's future might be in the hands of a criminal who now thought of Jim as a nephew.

"You should spend some time with Mom, Cait. I think it would be a healthy diversion for both of you at this point."

"I'm all right, Da," Caitlin said. "Mom and I have a history of stoking coals, not in a healthy way. She'd look at me, and I'd cry, then I'd look at her, and she would cry. Besides, I don't want to leave my students now. They'll provide all the diversion I need." Caitlin rolled the wineglass stem between her fingers and then thought she would change the subject. "Tell me how Garda Brenda Flaherty is doing."

Declan smiled at the mention of Brenda and said, "I wouldn't want to be anyone working for Mercer right now, especially Doug

Henson. If Brenda had a score to settle before, she now thinks she has a lifetime mission to take them down."

Declan was thinking that Enda McDonough needed to watch his step too.

"Hah!" Blurted Caitlin. "I never believed the story that you and she were the victims of a simple drone accident. Mercer and company tried to kill you, didn't they?"

"Well, some of their hired goons did, if you must know," said Declan.

Caitlin's remark gave him an idea. He was thinking he could get Brenda to put some heat on Enda—maybe enough to find his drug stash. Enda might feel guilty about ratting her out to Henson, perhaps guilty enough to make mistakes. Those mistakes might also lead to the undoing of Sabo and friends.

CHAPTER 26

Abu Aldhiyb, a.k.a. Wolf, had his goons haul Jim before him a second time.

With feigned largesse, he told Jim, "I'm gratified that your family has agreed to meet my demands so quickly. I am advised that the money will be wired to my account as requested. Now I'm sorry I did not ask for much more."

"I think you will get much more," said Jim, "but it won't be money."

Jim glanced at a pitcher of water on the table and hoped he would be offered a drink. He was not.

Wolf tightened his grip on the dagger hanging at his side then pulled it from the case and jabbed it into the table top.

"You may be right, Dr. Foley. We have detected some activity beyond the camp perimeter—lights and sounds. I think you and I should prepare to leave."

Jim tried to think of something, anything to stall Wolf, even a little.

"I would like to retrieve my notes, if you don't object. It won't take me long to put them together."

"Go ahead. Such dedication." Wolf waved his hand dismissively, indicating Jim should get on with it quickly. "Be back here in five minutes, or there will be a few of your fingers left on the table to greet our visitors."

Jim considered this threat to be an idle one at this point. He was sure Wolf would not want to hamper his escape with a wounded, bleeding hostage. He would want to keep Jim intact at least as long as it took to verify that he got his ransom money.

It was getting dark when Jim returned to the prison building. He thought any attempt to raid the camp would come at night, probably this night. He didn't know what kind of defenses were put in place to deter attackers, so he had no idea what to expect. He wasn't able to assemble all his notes before he was again hauled out to face Wolf. In the distance, a drone was winding up, and men were hustling items out to the cargo hatch.

Beyond the perimeter of Wolf's camp, Sadiq resigned himself to the fact that he was extra baggage and would be left behind while Henson and his men raided the camp. Henson had the earmarks of a sociopath and harbored no empathy for Sadiq. Strangely though, he felt the tiniest amount of affection for him because Sadiq was Jim's friend. Henson cared about Jim Foley—a man he barely knew—as if he was his own son. Henson puzzled over this feeling and attributed it to the fact that he made a promise to Bob Foley to rescue Jim. This was curious too; he ignored promises before, but somehow this was different.

Sadiq ambled painfully over to Henson and said, "You're going to leave me here, aren't you?" His eyes showed that he knew the answer to his question.

"You're not going to make it, my friend, and we can't get you to medical safety. What do you want me to do?" Henson asked.

"Help me into the drone, and I will fly it into the camp—my original plan. I will create the diversion for you," Sadiq said.

Henson was impressed by the heroic gesture; not what he thought would happen. He agreed and took him to the damaged drone, where Sadiq punched in the coordinates and started the engines.

"Perfect," said Henson as he drew his laser pistol up and pointed it at the back of Sadiq's head. The sound of the laser could not be heard above the engines, but death was instantaneous; Sadiq crumpled over the controls, in one hand clutching a small silver ring which had symbols of five religions on it, evenly spaced. Sadiq knew this would be his last adventure and was taking no chances on missing the light at the tunnel's end. Henson set the power on Sadiq's HCL to build up beyond safety limits and sent the drone on its way. He then returned to the control console for his robot.

"I will tell Dr. Foley of your sacrifice."

The IF sensor on one of Wolf's scanners picked up the robot and blasted it with a staccato of lasers. At the same time, Sadiq's drone crashed in the middle of the campsite, and the HCL exploded in a cluster of light and heat. All the remaining IF scanners picked up the heat signal and blasted the drone with lasers, adding to the mayhem. In turn, Henson's men took out each of the remaining scanners with their HCLs. The whole scene lit up like daylight, and the camp was flooded with sparks from flaming embers and debris.

When things quieted a little, Henson and his two men slowly circled through the camp. Most of the fires and hot spots had winked out, but there was plenty of smoke. Sadiq's drone continued to blaze, cremating everything within and around it. There was no sign of human life, but to be sure, Henson scanned the site with his remote. The IF sensor on his console picked up two small spots in one of the structures erected near a group of acacia trees and scrubby plants. *This could be nothing*, he thought, but he sent one of his men to check it out.

Two women dressed in plain black clothing with covered heads and faces were brought to Henson, young, spare, very frightened creatures who indicated in Arabic that they were taken hostage months earlier from a gypsy camp. They had been sexually abused and assigned custodial chores. It seemed they didn't consider themselves rescued so much as trading one abusive warden for another. Henson made no effort to dissuade them of this notion and sent them back to his drone to await instructions.

Henson wrapped a bandanna around his face and walked to the battery charging station, which was sputtering and billowing smoke. Wolf had sabotaged this facility before he departed, robbing him of the resource needed to recharge his drone. His drone didn't have the capacity to continue the pursuit, with barely enough to return to Mercer's site.

The water supply was left intact, which was not unusual. No one who lived or worked in the desert would intentionally ruin or despoil a water supply, not even bandits. Water was sacrosanct, and the concrete tank, half-buried in the sand, adjacent to a dried streambed still contained a potable though slightly alkaline supply. His men topped up the tanks in the drone and finished packing items, which they foraged from the campsite and considered useful. Henson retrieved the religious icon from the charred hand of Sadiq. Surprisingly, it did not melt in the fire—probably protected by Sadiq's grip. He thought he would give this to Jim Foley, as a memento of his friend, without mentioning the fact that he was the one who dispatched Sadiq. The option that he would not find Foley alive wasn't even in his bandwidth.

Henson tried to contact Mercer on the drone radio but got nothing but static. The communications tower near the campsite may have been disabled by Wolf and his men, so he decided to check it out. When he arrived at the tower, he could see, glinting in the setting sun, that a satellite dish near the top was bent toward the ground; and wires at the base were pulled out and dangling. He sent one of his men up to fix it, assuming that the guy would figure out what needed to be done. The repair wasn't perfect, but at least the connection had fewer interruptions.

Henson was able to contact Mercer and bring him up-to-date on the situation.

"I need to tell you," Mercer said. "One of my contacts with the Libyan State Police told me that you're a wanted man. The Gardai, the FBI, Interpol, everybody is looking for you. Thanks to Scarlet Kelly, you're number one on the shit list. You need to remove yourself from that list." Mercer paused, and before Henson could respond, he added, "What about that crispy, fried corpse in the drone? Any chance of planting something of yours on that body to throw off the scent?"

"That might work with the Libyans, but it would only slow the others up until their forensics kicked in. It's not a bad idea though. I got nothing else."

Henson thought that Mercer would consider him an increasing liability, and he would have to watch his back. Even so, he was

Mercer's best chance of getting Jim Foley back in one piece and was safe for a while.

"How are you going to do this?" Mercer asked. "Any identification you leave with the body will have to be burned to a frazzle, hence useless for the purpose."

"There is one way," Henson said. "I could place my HCL near the body. It will blacken after I restart the embers, but the engraved serial number will identify it as belonging to me at Mercer Enterprises."

Henson and Mercer ended their call, satisfied with the plan for now and anxious to get the police off Henson's trail and on to Wolf's. Henson soon found though that a fire in the drone could not be started without the addition of some kind of fuel and an accelerant to burn it. The HCL would not be convincing unless it looked as if it went through as much fire as the body. It had to be thoroughly blackened.

Henson decided that the addition of rags and petrol could be suspicious to investigators. A better method would be to flame the HCL with another laser pistol before he threw it near the body, so this was what he did. The night had turned pitch black by the time he completed the job, and he turned to his drone, now with two additional passengers ready for the journey to Mercer's site. The women could replace two of Mercer's custodial people who were killed in Wolf's earlier attack and get some cleanup done before Mercer and the Libyan cops arrived at the site.

CHAPTER 27

W olf rented three rooms at the Benghazi Ritz Amaz, one directly below his primary base of operations and the third for Jim Foley and his two guards. He outfitted the room below his primary base with a net stretched across the balcony and canted toward the inside. The room above didn't have a balcony, but the outside wall had a large window with no screen. He kept two guards in this room, who normally stayed close. But this time, things were different.

It was September 30 at 1630 when Wolf checked the balance in his Swiss account, and it showed a lodgment of ten million euros. He had previously arranged with the bank to have the funds immediately available by virtue of a large initial deposit. Wolf now logged into this account and had all the funds transferred to a different account. Law enforcement might get a subpoena to convince the reluctant Swiss, but they would find the account empty.

Wolf did plan to release Jim Foley, but not until he made good on his complete disappearance. Right now, he was ready to celebrate and planned to meet with his lady friend, Nadia, in a restaurant off the hotel lobby.

Following the meal, Wolf arranged to meet with Nadia later in his room. He left the restaurant with the remains of a bottle of very expensive champagne and two glasses. When he arrived, he was surprised to see the door to his room unlocked by virtue of being slightly ajar.

Breathing nervously into his mobile, he called his guards to tell them to return at once. There was no response, and each number called went to voice mail. Wolf had a small HCL pistol strapped to his ankle, but he thought it would be more of a distraction if he entered the room holding the champagne and glasses.

Doug Henson was sitting inside, silhouetted in front of the balcony with an HCL trained on Wolf.

"How thoughtful, you sleazy bastard. Are we going to drink to your capture and eventual death?"

"Meatface Henson," glowered Wolf. "I thought Mercer would have gotten rid of you by this time. How the hell did you find me?"

"I'm good at what I do. That's why Mercer keeps me around," said Henson. "You're only half Arab—the bottom half at that. I knew you wouldn't stick it out in the desert. All I had to do was check out the best hotels in Benghazi, and I knew I'd eventually find you. Five dudes traveling with a fair-haired, fair-skinned American is memorable." Henson gently waved the barrel of the HCL and pointed to a tabletop personal computer by the wall. "I'm going to turn you into a piece of charcoal if you don't bring up your account on that terminal right now. I want to see a recent deposit with a ten, followed by six zeroes."

"Why should I do that, Meatface?" said Wolf. "You're going to kill me either way, so why should I pay you to do it?"

"I will let you go if you turn over the ransom and Jim Foley," said Henson, concealing his lie with a poker face.

Wolf put the glasses on the table but held on to the champagne bottle. Nadia had arrived at the door and saw that it was ajar. She overheard some of the conversation inside and knew that Wolf was in trouble. She drew an HCL from her handbag, set it to low, and waited for an opportunity to push the door open.

Nadia fired instantly at Henson, but the shot burned into the chair inches from his head. She never got a second shot because Henson fired at her chest, drilling a fatal hole, which left the smoke and scent of burning flesh. Wolf thought to get his ankle weapon, but the encumbrance of the champagne bottle and the agility of Henson made him hesitate too long.

Henson turned his gaze on Wolf and said, "Nice try, Wolf. But that was your last card."

He waved the barrel of the HCL at the computer again.

Wolf was stunned as he looked at the fallen body of the woman he had planned to spend a great deal of time with following his escape. He poured himself a glass of champagne and silently toasted Nadia. Then reluctantly he took a small paper from his pocket, brought up his bank website on the computer, and punched in some numbers. Henson, looking over his shoulder, handed Wolf another slip of paper.

"Now transfer ten million euros to this number, Mercer's international account."

Henson waited through a succession of security protocols while the pistol grip turned sweaty in his hand. Finally, he read, "Transfer Completed," on the screen.

"Okay, Meatface, you've got my money." Wolf said. "I'll call this room from the lobby and give you Foley's whereabouts."

"Sorry, Wolf. I promised Mercer I'd rid the world of a cancer when I got this assignment. You're going to join your girlfriend."

Mercer leveled his HCL at Wolf's head.

Wolf flung the champagne bottle at Henson, who fired wild into the air through the open window. Wolf was able to get to the window before Henson could fire a second time. In a flash he jumped through the window just as Henson fired. The shot dissipated in the air as before. Wolf hit the net below, rolled off, and scampered through the room.

By the time Henson realized what happened, Wolf made good his escape. Henson ran into the hall to check the lift, but it wasn't moving. He opened the Exit door, looked down the stairs, but saw and heard nothing. He imagined Wolf took another lift or set of stairs and would be long gone. Actually, Wolf went topside to the hotel roof and left in a drone.

Henson returned to the room and pulled Nadia's body into a closet. He then went to the computer and transferred the ten million from the Mercer account (to which he had complete access) to his own personal account. That done, he grabbed the champagne bottle from the floor and poured the remains into the second glass.

"Not bad," he murmured. "I'll bet that set him back."

Henson called the front desk on the house phone.

"This is Carl Parker in Room 605. My boss wants to settle the account for all the rooms he rented and will pick up his receipt on the way out. He said to use the card number he gave you."

"Yes, sir, Mr. Parker. That would be for Rooms 605, 505, and 503?"

The clerk heard a mumbled affirmative as Henson was busy wiping prints from the bottle and glasses and elsewhere in the room. He grabbed the computer and left.

Room 505 was directly below 605, and Henson gained admittance by heating the lock to failure with a low setting on his HCL. Unfortunately, the smoke from the burning jamb set off a detector in the corridor, which in turn triggered the detectors on the whole floor and lit a warning light at the front desk.

The door to Room 503 burst open, and two men stepped out holding HCLs. Henson knew they had to be Wolf's goons assigned to guard Jim Foley. He drilled them both with two laser blasts and picked up their weapons. He found Jim Foley inside the room with his hands bound.

"Boy, am I glad to see you. I'm sick of goat meat and rice and wine tasting like it was filtered through some old socks," Jim said.

"Do you have a bag or suitcase?" Henson said as he untied Jim. Jim pointed to the closet. "Put your stuff in it, and let's get out of here."

When Jim had packed, Henson threw in the computer and three HCLs. They made their way down the stairs to the lobby amid the cacophony of noise from the detector alarms.

Jim and Henson had no difficulty slipping past the melee of guests, firemen, and police on the ground floor. Civilians were encouraged to exit the hotel as quickly as possible, and they made their way straight to a cab in the line outside.

At the airport, Jim was booked on a flight to Cork. Henson said he was remaining in Benghazi and wished him a safe return.

"Tell your father I already got my reward," he said as Jim tried again to thank him. He handed Jim the religious icon which he took from Sadiq. "I thought you might like this to remember your friend. Unfortunately, he didn't survive."

Before Jim could say anything, Henson left with a laundry bag containing the computer and HCLs.

Jim was very grateful to be heading home with his skin intact but couldn't help thinking what a strange man Doug Henson was. He didn't know that any ransom was paid or, in fact, if any kind of a deal was made for his release. He ordered a Bloody Mary from the flight attendant and tried not to think about Sadiq. He turned his thoughts to Caitlin, and suddenly things were a lot brighter and the details of his time in the desert less important.

Henson had apparently told no one about the release, so there was no one to greet Jim when he arrived in Cork. He stepped off the plane, dirty and unshaven, and collected his tattered belongings. The trauma of persons being killed around him started to take a toll, and he felt faint. He wondered if any of the families had been notified or, indeed, if all the bodies had been discovered. He studied the small religious token from Sadiq and wondered what the entire experience really meant.

CHAPTER 28

Sarah Benjamin arrived at Sham Rock, fatigued by the trip from Cork. It wasn't the distance so much as the battle she always had second-guessing the self-driving software. It seemed like turns would be made at the last minute, and the car would slow down or stop for no good reason. Most of Sarah's travel was on commercial carriers, so she didn't drive much and never warmed to the idea of turning control over to robots. Still, she wasn't a Luddite so much as an antiquarian. The rural character of Ireland was the subject of much of the artwork in her gallery, and she didn't want to see it threatened.

The Irish road system would become increasingly difficult to navigate by an aging population or, in fact, by any component of the population. As years passed, both the Irish and European governments were left with two choices: upgrade the infrastructure to deal with the vehicles or upgrade the vehicles to deal with the infrastructure. The island was too small, too storied by the diaspora, too hung up on a tourist economy to entertain a major tear up, straightening, resurfacing, widening, modernization. Besides, it was a lot cheaper to upgrade to self-driving cars and drones because the costs would be borne by drivers, not the government. Also, vehicles would be upgraded anyway; it was inevitable.

Sarah was dying for a cup of tea, and Bob Foley brought a tray of biscuits.

"I was thinking of this moment all morning, Bob—a bracing cup of tea and a few biscuits, in your company, of course."

"Of course," said Bob, who was wearing a blue apron stained with acrylic paint. He kissed her warmly, greatly relieved to see her after his ordeal with all the events surrounding Jim's kidnapping.

Sarah wanted to see the portrait that Bob was working on but also get an update on Jim, who wanted to return to work almost immediately. Bob thought Jim should take some time off after his rescue, and Sarah and Caitlin agreed. When Jim was told that his father paid out ten million of his newfound wealth to get him back, he was overcome with rage and not inclined to hang about and stew.

"So how is Jim doing since he went back to work?" Sarah asked.

"He feels guilty about costing me a fortune I never really had," said Bob. "I told him to burn incense for old Sham because—thanks to him—I don't have to hang Bob's framed fingers over the mantelpiece."

"That's disgusting," Sarah said. "Do you think that criminal would really have chopped off Jim's fingers?"

"Are you kidding? He burned holes through at least six Libyans. Declan told me the authorities say it was a guy they call Wolf. If I ever get my hands on him, he'll be baying at the moon in pain because his balls will be missing." Bob started to put his painting materials away, but he kept the portrait he was working on covered. "Sorry, Sarah, I'm letting him continue to get to me."

"You don't want me to see the portrait you're working on because you haven't been working on it, right?" said Sarah. "Too distracted, shall we say?"

"You know," Bob continued, "Jim said Mercer spoke to him only briefly since he returned from Libya. According to Jim, Mercer was very glad he was returned safely but said very little about the rescue. Mercer said the project was successful, and OT would have a big check coming. I said nothing to Jim, but I think I know why Mercer was so terse. Declan told me Henson disappeared—never returned to Mercer Enterprises. Also, Jim said Henson wanted me to know that 'he got his reward.' What do you think that means?"

"Wow!" said Sarah. "This guy Henson got his hands on the ransom money? If that's the case, Bob, you did cut Wolf's balls off, or at least Henson did."

The conversation was broken when Bob's mobile rang.

"Hi, Declan. Say, I'm glad you had dinner with Jim and Caitlin, and sorry I couldn't join you. Sarah and I had this weekend planned for a while and…"

"No explanations necessary," interrupted Declan. "I'll catch you up when I see you. Just wanted you to know that I just heard from the Libyan police. They said they found Henson's body at a campsite in the desert that Wolf was using, the body burned so badly that they had to use Henson's HCL for identification."

"Wait," Bob said, "if Henson was killed in Libya, that had to have happened after he rescued Jim. When did the Libyans say they found the body?"

"That's the problem, Bob," said Declan. "The body was found just a day after Henson released Jim. The timing doesn't add up. Henson couldn't have gotten from Benghazi to the desert camp that fast. I'm thinking I need to go down there and check things out."

"Yeah, Dec," Bob said. "I'd hate to think my millions got burned up with Henson."

"No fear of that, Bob," Declan said. "Mercer says the ransom money was lodged to his account then transferred to another account shortly after, probably owned by Henson. Looks like your bro got the ten million, jumped ship, was killed, and left his ill-begotten gains behind."

"Not a surprise," Bob said. "If you find he's still alive, you guys can add theft to suspicion of murder, attempted murder, and drug-trafficking. One way or another, Mercer should be glad to be rid of him. He's gotten to be a real liability."

"I hate to say it, Bob," said Declan. "We owe him for getting Jim back to us. I think Caitlin would give the son of a bitch a big kiss if he were still around. Nevertheless, if he's not really dead, we're going to nail his ass, bro or not."

"I had a strange feeling the last time I saw him," said Bob. "He had an unusual amount of interest in the picture of my birth father, and I promised him a copy if he got Jim back."

Bob ended the call by saying that he hoped Declan would be very careful if he went to Libya.

Sarah had been in the kitchen and now returned with another pot of tea and fixings.

"We need a change of venue, Bob," she said. "Let's discuss your Sham Rock renovation project."

"Actually, Sarah, I have to I tell you honestly. I wouldn't have done it if I knew what I was getting into," Bob said. "You know from your work on the gallery that every renovation to a building's exterior, or even a demolition, requires a blessing and license from the council in the county which has jurisdiction for the site of the project. This in itself is not so unusual. The democratic notion of it sounds reasonable, but the execution is byzantine."

"What do you mean, Bob?" said Sarah. "Don't you have your zoning laws in the States?"

"That's just it," said Bob. "Zoning laws apply to everyone in the region uniformly. Council decisions are subjective, arbitrary, influenced by all manner of things, including the resources and political influence of every one of your neighbors who might have some 'problem' with whatever it is that you're doing. It's a setup ripe for graft, not that I would accuse anyone on the Cork Council of such."

"No one objected to the work you did on Sham Rock, Bob, though I admit most of it was inside the house." Sarah sipped her cup cautiously, not wanting to set Bob off on a tirade.

"Then why all the paperwork and months to get approval? But the worst part, Sarah, was trying to get stuff done from the States communicating by e-mail and dealing with time zones. Stitch asked me the same questions repeatedly because my responses were written on scraps of paper and stuffed in his toolbox. He has no office other than his shirt pocket or toolbox."

Bob turned on the television but muted the sound. Sarah took the remote and switched to a channel which showed herds of elk traveling the northern expanses of Canada.

"Look at that, Bob, they were just put on the endangered species list—right below us."

"We're not on that list yet, sweet face, thanks to people like my son. But back to the subject at hand," said Bob. "A lot of the reason things are done this way over here is that 'they' want to discourage any kind of change to this land of legend. It's been that way for years and will continue so into the future."

"Don't blame the poor folks over here, Commander Foley," said Sarah. "Most of the Irish with some kind of stake in this country reside elsewhere—the famous Irish diaspora. Ireland is a place in their memories, a sacred, unchanging place. They come here as tourists and want to see no castle stone unturned and every chunk of lichen in place."

"You're probably right," said Bob. "Heritage and history are important, but a happy middle ground must be found. I don't pretend to know what it is, but I can tell you I know one thing for sure that can be changed with benefits all around."

Sarah leaned over to him, and very close to his face said, "Tell me about it."

"Asphalt shingle roofs, or solar tile roofs. They're so much better in so many ways than putting tons of clay and concrete on top of a house…"

Focused as he was on Sarah's proximity, Bob was distracted by the elk on the telly. A great bull was nudging his rack against a younger rival and pushing him away from a female in heat. Finally, with a thrust energized by the strength in his loins, he put the young buck to rout. The female stopped and turned, lowered her back, and spread her haunches. Bob shut off the telly and pulled Sarah toward the bedroom. She went with him willingly.

CHAPTER 29

Enda McDonough was pushing small, buttered potatoes around on his plate. He was distracted after visiting his mother at the nursing home. Even though she was incapacitated and barely able to string words together, he sorely missed her company, particularly at mealtimes. She would dredge out a picture of him as a small boy and gently run her fingers across the tiny image. Somehow, when he watched her do that, he thought his life could still be different in many wonderful ways; would be different. Such fantasies, even though brief, were preferable to the monk-like solitude his life was becoming.

Enda glanced at the newspaper and saw that the *Fancy Fran* yacht would be back in Kinsale by week's end. A contingent of Arabs would be onboard, eager for some shark-fishing. The marina was going to be very busy, and he saw a chance to crew on one of the shark boats. This was just the change of pace he needed, since his drug supplies were low, and customers were going elsewhere.

Sabo told him that Doug Henson left the employ of Mercer without a word to anyone, and Con Mercer was royally pissed. Sabo was angling for Henson's job as head of security, so far unsuccessfully. When Mercer realized that Henson transferred the ransom money from his account, he thought of sending Sabo to find Henson and kill him for real. Mercer, however, thought Henson would get the better of that confrontation. Sabo knew that getting Henson would put him in solid with Mercer, but he wasn't eager for the confrontation either.

There seemed to be no way around it; without a connection to Mercer, Enda had no source for lyminiol supplies or any other drugs.

He hoped Sabo would get the job with Mercer even though he didn't much like him. Better the devil you know, and all that.

Meanwhile, Enda called several of his fishing contacts and found that Herman Gully and his brothers would be interested in taking him on, provided he didn't ask for time off to go to a funeral. He was tempted to tell Gully to "Feck off," but he suppressed the urge. The Gullys had drones on their boats, which they used to search the Atlantic for signs of shark and drop chum as bait. The drones were equipped with vanadium cobalt batteries, which could stay aloft for days if need be. Enda was one of the few fishermen in Kinsale who could service and troubleshoot these drones. He was thus assured of employment with one or another of the crews.

Garda Brannigan subsequently paid a visit to Enda, which was hardly social.

"Okay, Enda, it's time to pull up your socks and come on down to the station for a little chat."

"The hell you say," said Enda. "Are you going to enroll me in Kinsale's best retirement home?"

"Speaking of which," said Brannigan. "I hope your mum is doing fine. She has cross enough to bear with you as a son. Be it as it may, there's a person down at the station wants to see you, and it's not someone you want to ignore."

Enda grabbed a hat and jacket and said, "There's no one at the retirement home I'd care to see. And besides, if you want me to get in that car, you'll have to show me your driver's license."

"The car drives itself, you amadan," Brannigan said as he pushed Enda into the vehicle.

Enda didn't think it was Inspector McGuinness who wanted to see him. He already blew that interview but suspected this may be some kind of follow-up. He also didn't want to be seen going to the Gardai Station in case it got back to Sabo or one of his nasty friends. He pulled his cap down and crouched in the back seat.

Sergeant Pat Twomey was busy with a woman who wanted to renew her passport when Brannigan came in with Enda. Brannigan offered Enda a cup of tea and ushered him into a back room—the same room where he met earlier with Inspector McGuinness.

The door opened, and Garda Brenda Flaherty entered, holding a small package. Enda blanched as he recognized the same girl who previously showed him RTE credentials and expressed interest in his new crypt, also the same person he told Henson about.

"I don't know who you are this time, missy, but I have nothing to say to you."

"I'm Garda Brenda Flaherty of the drug squad, Mr. McDonough," said Brenda. "Call me Missy at your own peril. I'm told you had something to do with the attempt on my life at St. James's Hospital in Dublin. Maybe you'd like to know how I feel about that?"

Enda quickly denied any connection with the attempt on her life and swore he didn't know she was a cop.

"The only other person I told about our interview was Doug Henson. You need to talk to him, not me."

"Oh, I'll get to him soon enough. First, I want to show you some things that were found at Sham Rock, the Foley residence." Brenda carefully withdrew a small plastic packet from the package she was holding and placed it on the table. It contained a piece of cinnamon stick. "This was found in the passageway or tunnel leading from the house to the beach. The DNA found on it matches the DNA in your fisherman's registry. What were you doing in Sham Rock, Mr. McDonough?"

Enda hemmed and hawed and finally said, "I must have stepped in there, looking for something that might have been connected to Scarlet Kelly's death. Yeah, that's it. I forgot to mention it to the police."

"So you were definitely inside the Sham Rock tunnel," Brenda said. "Then you must have been the person who also left this in the tunnel." She threw a second packet onto the table. It contained a plastic coffee pod with a split at the top, edged in a white, powdery substance. "You know what this is, McDonough, because you've been pushing lyminiol around this area for years. Whose prints do you think are on this plastic?"

"I don't deal drugs," Enda said. "If my prints are on that, it's because I thought I was handling a coffee pod. I sometimes carry them around on the off chance..."

"I don't think a prosecutor is going to have a tough job convincing the judge that your off chance is pushing drugs," said Brenda. "How about, on the off chance, we do a little trade?" Her question was greeted with a long silence. "You tell me where Henson is, and we'll forget about the coffee pod. What do you say?"

"This is a railroad job," Enda said. "You planted that shit! You wouldn't be offering a trade if you didn't. Besides, it won't do you any good. I have no idea where Henson is. In fact, I heard he may be dead."

"Well, that's a problem for you. If you don't know where Henson is—living or dead—you're looking at a drug conviction. Unless, of course, you have something else of interest."

There was another long silence as Brenda scooped up the packets.

Brenda had previously rehearsed this whole scam with Declan McGuinness. On the assumption that Enda had been in the tunnel and was using it for storage when Bob Foley was back in the States, they crafted the bit about the two packets. It would only work if Enda thought the probability was high that they had the goods on him. It seemed to be working as Enda was now eager to find something to trade.

"Look," said Enda. "I really don't know the whereabouts of Henson, but I know he killed Scarlet Kelly."

Brenda was suddenly interested and pressed Enda for details.

Enda fished a fresh cinnamon stick from his pocket and was about to place it in his mouth when he changed his mind. He looked at the stick then put it back in his pocket. Enda described his meeting with Henson in the Dungeon.

"Henson said Scarlet threatened to reveal his drugs operation to the Gardai, and he blamed me for telling Scarlet about it in the first place."

"Did he tell you he killed Scarlet Kelly?" Brenda said.

"He as much as did. He said she met with an unfortunate accident, and if I told anyone about his drugs business, I'd be found on the beach in pieces—found on the beach like she was," Enda said.

Brenda pushed a pad and pen across the table to Enda and said, "Write it out, McDonough. All the details. Leave nothing out."

"How about the drug bust?" Enda asked.

"If your story helps us nail Henson, you're good," said Brenda. "But you're not off the hook yet. If you have a drug stash in Kinsale, we want it."

Brenda knew she was pushing her luck.

"Henson took whatever I had," Enda lied. "He took it away on the yacht. I got no stash."

Enda didn't want to tell the police anything, but he was secretly glad to pin something on Henson, whom he disliked and feared. Henson might, in fact, be dead and would no longer be supplying him with drugs, or anything, so nothing was lost.

CHAPTER 30

The moon was traversing its monthly path, as inexorably as ever, an old friend seeking the most comfortable cloud to nestle into. Sham Rock was bathed in silvery light as time and the process of healing progressed. Bob Foley was enjoying the night air and barely thinking about his son's ordeal or his missing millions. Life was pleasant, and the time he spent with Sarah made it even better.

Bob had been seeing Sarah as often as he could. He would even find himself inventing reasons for a visit, such as meeting at the gallery on Oliver Plunkett with her sister, Deb, to discuss his landscaping project. Deb knew what Bob was doing and was beginning to get annoyed at the amount of time Bob was taking to come to a decision on seemingly minor stuff. At one point, he told Deb he wanted to see a 3D image of her plan in the special lighting that was available at the gallery. She decided at that point that Bob needed a wrenching distraction.

The subject of Doug Henson making off with Bob's millions was never discussed out of deference to Bob's feelings. Even though Henson's theft was eclipsed by Jim Foley's rescue, the time had come for a different rejoinder. Deb decided Bob should deal with the issue of Henson and his love-hate relationship with the thief and killer. One day she confronted him at the gallery when Sarah was out running errands.

"There's nothing I can do about Henson," Bob said. "My money is not a top priority for the police. It insulates him and gives him plenty of reason to keep a low profile. His drug connections have dried up. He doesn't need them anymore. What do you want me to do—hire a private detective?"

"You should get Mercer to do it. Henson probably owes him too. Mercer has resources neither you nor the police have," Deb said.

"You've got to be kidding, Deb. Do you think Mercer would return my money if he got his hands on it?"

Bob didn't expect Deb to answer his question. He knew this whole subject was out of her element.

Back at Sham Rock, enjoying the night, Bob was thinking anew about Deb's suggestion. She was correct in assuming that he was not dealing with the issue of the ransom money. He never had his mitts on a single euro of that money and didn't at some level consider it a reality. But it was real, and Doug Henson, his "bro," stole it from him. It was not intended to be Henson's reward for extricating his son from a life-and-death situation. He would gladly have rewarded Henson, but only after both his son and the money were returned.

Bob decided to call Declan. He would know how to handle this. Sure, getting Jim back was the priority, as it should be in a kidnapping situation. But getting Henson had to now be a prime objective for Declan who would want him for questioning about the murder of Scarlet Kelly and the attempt on Garda Flaherty's life.

"We need to talk, Dec. I want to ask you about Henson and the not inconsiderable sum he escaped with. I want to discuss my options."

"I can't get down to Kinsale til tomorrow evening, Bob," Declan McGuinness said. "Why don't we meet at the Dungeon for dinner at 6:30? On me. I'll stay over if you don't mind, as I've got business at the station in the morning."

Bob was agreeable but refused Declan's offer to buy his meal, saying, "I'm the deep pockets here, and besides, I'll be the one that's asking for free advice."

Bob furrowed his brow and decided there was one more call he wanted to make before he turned in. He punched in Con Mercer's private mobile number and waited through several rings. Finally, a slurry voice lubricated with whiskey answered.

"Mr. Foley," Mercer said. "I'm so glad you called me. We haven't talked since your son was rescued, and I wanted to tell you how overjoyed I am for your family."

"Your joy is overshadowed by your lack of an apology for putting him in harm's way in the first place," Bob said. "Your own crooked security chief warned you not to leave Jim in the desert for months without adequate protection."

"Why are you calling me, Mr. Foley?" Mercer said. "I am not responsible for Doug Henson stealing your ransom payment. Frankly, I'm amazed that a man of your modest means had the resources to pay such a high ransom. You should have negotiated it down to a smaller amount, which I'm sure the kidnapper would have accepted." Realizing what he just said, Mercer quickly backpedaled. "Of course, no one can put a monetary value on human life, but the bandits quickly learned that neither my company nor Ocean Tech would meet their demands. They had to know they would have to settle for less. That's all I'm saying."

"I wouldn't expect you to understand," Bob said. "Everything to you is a business transaction. You have no children and cherish little else besides money."

"I repeat," said Mercer, "why are you calling me?"

"I want justice," said Bob. "I know you're not happy with what Henson did either. I want to know everything about that guy—the stuff that's not in his police record."

"I already told the police everything," said Mercer as he punched his phone off.

Bob was now becoming more convinced that he would need to hire a good private investigator, someone who knew how to follow a trail, sniff out details, and extract blood from a stone. Declan could help with this. He knew the Gardai occasionally employed contract investigators to supplement their resources. These guys would be expensive, but thanks to Otis Sham, he could afford to do it. He could spend a few thousand to chase the millions Henson would have tucked away. Bob finally went to bed with the germ of a plan in his mind. Out through the window, high over the Bandon River, the moon was emerging from behind a large gray cloud. Bob took this as an omen that he was on the right track.

Sarah Benjamin called in the morning. She just returned from an exhibition in Brussels and was anxious to catch up on events since her absence.

"Deb says you may finally be coming to grips with the fact that you were ripped off for ten million euros."

"Well, not really, Sarah," Bob said. "I can't miss something I never had, so to speak. What upsets me is the scale of the injustice. I don't know if Henson planned to abscond with the ransom money from the beginning. I think he genuinely wanted to rescue Jim, but the money was an irresistible windfall."

"Do you think he knew where you got the money? I mean, do you think he knew about Otis Sham?" Sarah said.

"The find of gold coins was in the paper, but the value wasn't mentioned," Bob said. "Henson may have guessed it. That would make the theft from his 'bro' even easier to rationalize. It wasn't exactly 'hard-earned' money."

"I think he suspects it came from Mercer or Ocean Tech. Doesn't matter. He's a bad dude who needs to be caught. And what's left of your money should be returned to you." Sarah quickly changed the subject. "Deb says you really miss me when I'm gone."

"Just a little," Bob said. "The good thing is that you always return. When are you coming down to check my latest etchings?"

"If you will let me see the portrait you're working on, I'll be down tomorrow," Sarah said.

"Since you promise to show up, I'll tell you about the portrait," said Bob. "It's a painting of my birth father, which I made from the old photo JJ gave me. I left the beard off, figuring to add it later. Guess what? The resemblance to me is uncanny."

"Then I should love it, Bob," said Sarah. "As you know, sometimes portraits are more revealing than the physical reality. Maybe I'll spot something in it even you missed."

Later that evening, Bob checked the internet to see if the Dungeon had any specials planned. Turns out they would be hosting a guest chef for a "Taste of India" all-week event. This looked good to Bob who remembered a pleasant Navy assignment he once had in

Delhi. He would order the mildest thing on the menu and wash it down with cold ale, perhaps a tandoori shrimp with rice.

Bob handed Declan a Jameson and soda as he stepped in the door at six.

"We're doing Indian cuisine tonight, Dec. I hope you like your dinner spicy. But if not, you can still order from the regular menu."

"If you can do it, so can I," Declan said.

CHAPTER 31

A greeter at the door to the Dungeon dressed in Indian garb handed out menus for the "Taste of India" specials. Declan asked a few questions and was assured that if he didn't order any of the items with the little red fire-engine logo, he would be fine. They stepped inside and were quickly ushered to one of the usually dimly lit tables.

"This chef has a five-star rating, Dec," Bob said. "You're going to like the cuisine. Follow my lead and taste how savory they can make the veggies with their combination of spices and clay oven cooking. They have some crossover things on the menu too. These combine Western and Indian recipes in a very creative way. I haven't tried these before, but I'm tempted."

"The stuff certainly smells tasty enough," Declan said as he watched the steaming trays gliding past him. "Before I get lost in your epicurean ramblings, though, you need to get yourself another drink and get ready for what I have to tell you."

"Why is it that every time I come to the Dungeon, I feel as though I'm about to be confronted with some existential issue?" Bob said rhetorically.

"What do you expect?" said Declan. "You're eating gourmet food surrounded by torture devices. I don't know the owner, but he must have a strange sense of irony."

"Okay, Declan, what do you have to tell me?" Bob was now drinking his cocktail in a defensive manner, without a clue as to what would be coming next from across the table.

"Bob, I've been talking to some experts—geneticists, biologists. Your DNA lines up so closely with Doug Henson that you could be taken for identical twins. If Henson hadn't got his face so scarred up, we wouldn't be able to tell you apart," Declan said.

"How could we be twins, Dec? He's older than me by a couple of years."

Bob reached into his pocket and took out the picture of his birth father, whose name he did not know. He studied it again for the umpteenth time. He again wondered if the writing on the back, "Graystone," could be a surname.

"That's exactly right. That leaves only one possibility. Doug Henson and you are clones," said Declan, speaking slowly for emphasis.

"Dec, are you trying to blow my fucking mind? Because if you are, you've succeeded. How could anyone be so narcissistic or arrogant that he would clone himself, rather than father, a child in the normal way? Bob was truly puzzled. If Henson and I are somebody's clone, why are we so different?"

"First," said Declan. "I don't know why your birth father wanted to clone himself. I suppose we'll never know that. Your original birth record, if there ever was one, was probably sealed or destroyed when you were legally adopted by JJ. Your mother was a surrogate who contributed none of her DNA to you. It's quite possible that Henson's mother was a different surrogate."

"As to why Henson is or was a murderer, thief, and drug smuggler and you are a boring, retired Navy commander, that's all about nurture, not DNA," continued Declan. "But you know that."

"Give me some time and a little more whiskey, and maybe I can deal with this," Bob said. "But I realize what you're saying. Having the same DNA doesn't make Henson my brother. Relationships make brothers, and Henson and I never had a relationship. Also, I have to say at this point that I don't think we ever would."

"Just the same, don't underestimate the power of DNA, Bob," Declan said. "I once knew three brothers who separated as adults and led their own lives independent of one another. Years later, they all met at a reunion and discovered that each had built a fountain in the backyard of their home. They couldn't explain why, but each felt compelled to do this."

"That's anecdotal bullshit," returned Bob. "I can't accept that Henson and I had the same motivations. He had more in common with the guy that kidnapped Jim. That's why he was able to track him down so quickly. Henson was a stone-cold killer, and I, as you well know, am a sweet and lovable curmudgeon."

"Undoubtedly," said Declan. "But look around you, at some of the torture devices modeled in here. You can bet some sweet and lovable guys had no problem designing and testing them once upon a time."

The Indian cuisine arrived, and Declan braced himself for a bout with curry and peppers. He decided to start with a cold swig of ale.

Along one side of the dining room, a slight man in his twenties walked purposefully toward Bob and Declan's table.

"Are you Bob Foley?" he said.

Bob nodded, and the man handed him an envelope. He left before Bob completed opening the envelope. Bob didn't read the computer-printed note inside but saw the signature at once: D. H.

"Wait," shouted Bob, who looked at Declan. "It's from Henson!"

Declan spun around, leapt to his feet, and chased after the young man. He grabbed the man's arm as he reached for his ID.

"I'm Inspector McGuinness with the Gardai. Who gave you this envelope?"

"A guy stopped me outside, offered me a tenner to deliver an envelope to a Bob Foley, showed me this picture." The man handed a small photo of Bob to Declan. "I don't know who he was."

"Stay here," Declan said and rushed outside, searching in several directions for anyone that might be Henson or one of his goons.

The twilight made it difficult to discern things clearly, but he did see and hear a motorcycle in the distance. Far out on the Bandon River, he saw a drone rising in the gathering fog with the unmistakable but barely audible hum of four Lundies.

Back inside the Dungeon, the man gave a description of an old, bearded man but couldn't offer anything else. It wasn't Henson, but it could have been someone he enlisted. Declan let the messenger go and returned to his table.

"How did he know I'd be here? We didn't say anything to any-one, Dec." Bob handed the note to Declan.

"He was probably watching this place for a while. He knew you liked it. Hell, Henson liked it too. I told you about that DNA thing—mysterious vibrations or something." Declan read the note aloud, "The note says you owe Henson a photo and to take a picture of it and e-mail it to him. What's he talking about?"

Bob explained his meeting with Henson and the promise to exchange the photo for Henson's help in rescuing Jim.

"This message could have been sent by Henson before he was allegedly killed, but it's very suspicious. This is an Irish e-mail address. I can have my IT guys try to trace it. We might get lucky," Declan said.

"If he is still alive, I could also send him the DNA comparison analysis," said Bob. "That would tip him off that you have his DNA, making it easier for the police to catch him."

"Don't send anything to that address," said Declan. "Let who-ever sent that note think you didn't get it or you're ignoring it. Then you may get another contact. Besides, I can give his DNA to the medical examiner, and if I can retrieve some of that body in Libya, he can check it for a match. If there is no match, then we know Henson's still alive, and the note most likely did come from him."

Bob scanned the room, wary of any more possible interruptions to his dinner.

"My contractor, Stitch says that Otis Sham must have been some kind of leprechaun to have left me a pot of gold, but if he was, his gift had a short shelf life. Now that Jim is safe, I'd like to take some extra steps to get my windfall back."

"What did you have in mind?" Declan asked Bob. "Even if we caught Henson, he wouldn't be likely to give up the money. His attorneys would be the ones to get it."

"I'm thinking of hiring a private investigator, someone who spe-cializes in following money trails. What can you suggest about that?"

Bob finished his entrée and ordered rice pudding encrusted with brown sugar and cherry chips.

"It doesn't hurt to have additional resources," said Declan. "There's a good one in Dublin I can recommend, and he's part of a firm with offices in Paris, Brussels, Miami, and several other cities I can't remember offhand. He's done some work for us in the past. It would be expensive though. Let me make some calls."

Bob was surprised that Declan was so agreeable to the suggestion. He just assumed Declan would regard any mention of a private investigator as an inference of inefficiency on the part of the Gardai.

"What's his name, Dec?"

"I'll do you one better," Declan said, and he handed Bob a card which he extracted from his jacket pocket. The card read, "Peter Collins, PI, Barclays International." An address and phone number in Dublin were listed.

CHAPTER 32

B ob woke at the Rock in a state of mental confusion. The knowledge that he was cloned from someone who looked just like the image he saw in the mirror was enough to make his sleep sporadic and fitful. He could have blamed it on the Indian cuisine, but he knew better. Considering the differences between himself and his other clone, Doug Henson, he wondered if he was also radically different from his genetic parent. Or maybe—what was even more disconcerting to him—maybe he was more alike his parent and bro than he thought. Could he kill a beautiful girl like Scarlet Kelly and live with the knowledge, as apparently Henson did? Did his genetic parent have a murderous streak also?

Stitch Hegarty, his contractor, was scheduled to meet with Bob this morning. However, since Stitch was an adherent of "Irish time," the window for the meeting could stretch into the afternoon. He wondered what Stitch would think if he knew Bob was a clone. He imagined it would make no difference as long as Bob paid his invoices, a pile of which cluttered Bob's office files and e-mail box.

Stitch was currently working on a stretch of roof, replacing damaged cement tiles with newer but mismatched versions. The roof couldn't be seen easily, except by overflying hooded crows and pigeons, and it would be partially covered by the solar panels. Still, it was a time-consuming and expensive process, and Bob wondered that, even after decades, Ireland was still not into asphalt shingles. Stitch would say, "What good are they? They can't be very strong if you can cut them with shears." There was no arguing with him, and he always had the architect, Lord Blarney, on his side. Bob thought that with his newfound wealth, he could have the entire roof covered with solar panels designed to look like clay tiles. By that time, Bob could put all Stitch's kids through private colleges if he had kids.

Stitch finally arrived, late as usual, but smiling and happy to report that he found someone to work on the roof with him. Bob expressed his satisfaction with this news but wondered to himself why it had taken so long.

Each of the nation states of the Republic of Europe had established a labor broker with a registry of available talent. The acceptance of English as the common language of commerce was accompanied by the even more unlikely eventuality that building codes and regulations would be simplified and reduced from a humongous patchwork to a single set of volumes; that trade schools could agree on standardized, teachable practices and licensing parameters. With speedy, inexpensive transportation and a multitude of hostels available in each of the nation states, there was no reason for a legitimate construction project to languish for want of qualified talent—except for one thing.

Bob liked to refer to it as the WADILT syndrome: "We've always done it like that." The old-timers in Ireland didn't want a bunch of Poles and Germans working on their site, plotting and scheming among themselves, bringing in new and disruptive technology. Of course, this wasn't a situation unique to Ireland, and in fact, Irish veterans of the EDF were some of the more likely to brush away parochial paranoia and work together successfully with other Europeans. Stitch wasn't a veteran, but he did manage to hire a Pole; although he was a Pole who was born in Kinsale and lived there most of his life.

"What are you going to do about scallawag Sham's leprechaun cave?" Stitch asked Bob.

"Leave it as is for now, Stitch," said Bob. "If I ask you for a quote to fill it in, I'll be wanting my gold back once I read your figure."

Seemingly unamused, Stitch opined, "Oh well, the council would probably have to approve filling it in, and that could take months."

Stitch's attempt at humor fell flat when both men silently realized that the council potentates might, in fact, object—if they found out about it.

Most of the work Stitch did for Bob these days was based on a time and material estimate. These estimates had a way of creeping higher when unforeseen conditions or unplanned events cropped up, as was frequently the case. A tactic often used by Stitch was to cleverly suggest plausible, attractive alternatives that would offer something better for slightly more material expense but substantially more labor cost. Bob thought sometimes that he would be better off just putting Stitch on a retainer like a solicitor, or better yet, just give him dibs on his bank account.

"You know," said Stitch, pausing with a squint. "Your landscape designer, Deb Benjamin, could come up with some attractive plants to hide old Sham's cave, but the entrance door will still need sanding and painting with a matte finish color—"

Bob cut him off. He could picture his suggestion evolving into replacing the entire entrance door.

"Just give me a quote on removing the door and filling in the space, Stitch. And we won't worry about the council."

Bob knew he made a mistake as soon as the words left his mouth. Stitch smiled to himself as he contemplated a low estimate, which he could easily escalate for a variety of unforeseen conditions. A host of potential delays, like skip rental, dumping license, scrap-recycling, etc., could try Bob's patience, causing him to want the job done despite the cost.

"Wait," said Bob. "We'll just let it be for now."

Stitch was undeterred. He took this as an opportunity to work on Deb Benjamin—a not-unpleasant prospect. Eventually, Bob would come around.

While the two men were mulling the sculptural possibilities of the Sham Rock site, Bob's mobile rang.

"Peter Collins here. Inspector Declan McGuinness said you might be interested in my services. I'll be in Cork next week and could run over to Kinsale around one o'clock on Wednesday if you like."

A meeting was arranged, and Bob was told that Declan had filled in Peter with most of the details.

Bob ended the call and said beneath his breath, somewhat sardonically, "Another hand out for my gold. I can see old Otis laughing now."

Peter showed up on Wednesday afternoon in a red electric Ferrari. He had slicked-back blonde hair and sported a matching mustache, dark sunglasses, and a tweedy jacket. When he greeted Bob, his lined face and hands showed him to be older than he appeared at a distance.

Inside, Peter Collins settled into one of Bob's overstuffed chairs, declined a drink, and took out a small recorder, which he placed next to his resting hand.

"Bob—if I may call you that—I have no interest in 'catching' Doug Henson if he is indeed still alive. If I were to locate his whereabouts, which I expect I would do, I'd relay that information to law enforcement. My primary interest, if you become my client, will be to get back the money he stole from you, or what's left of it." He handed Bob a résumé containing a copy of his credentials and references, also a blank contract form, which detailed his expenses and payment arrangements.

Bob scanned the papers as Collins talked about his previous cases, work with the Gardai and other agencies, and success record.

"With all due respect for your probity and credentials, what's to stop you or one of your cohorts from finding the money and keeping it? We are talking millions here, and that's a big temptation."

"Good question," Peter said. "First, as detailed in the contract, I must have a sponsor in law enforcement—in this case, Inspector McGuinness of the Gardai. Second, my reports to you are copied to the inspector. Third, any stolen assets I find must be turned over to the Gardai before they can be released to you. True, I could scam these checkpoints, but as an employee of Barclays, I am subject to audit if I report that I failed to find any of your stolen assets."

"What would be our chances for success?" Bob asked, still not wholly convinced of the wisdom in using a PI.

"Before I could answer that question, I would need to ask you some questions of my own," Peter said. "But first you need to sign on as a client. Let me leave the paper with you, and I'll check back with you tomorrow. If you sign up and change your mind in a week, we'll tear up the contract."

Bob agreed, and Peter Collins shook hands and made a hasty departure. As the red Ferrari swept into the distance, Bob decided he would have the drink that Collins declined.

Bob read and reread the documents left with him. Finally, he called Declan on his mobile and told him about the meeting.

"I really can't tell you what to do, Bob," Declan said. "Collins is very good, but there's no guarantee he will find your money. His services are expensive, and if he comes up dry, you'll be out a lot of money."

The two men were silent for several seconds.

"Hell, Declan, I still have some of Otis's horde that Henson didn't get. I think I'm going to do it," Bob blurted. "Also, if Henson wants everyone to think he's dead, he'll be keeping a low profile, which means not spending big chunks of my money."

CHAPTER 33

Herman Gully's shark boats were strictly for work. The decks were slippery and smelled of fish. Varnish and paint were daubed on areas of woodwork that were damaged or rotted. The lack of adequate surface preparation resulted in lumpy and prematurely peeling paint. The metalwork was dull, pitted, and worn. By contrast, the fishing stations were decently appointed and the galleys clean and well-provisioned.

The Saudis and other foreigners were not looking for a tourist attraction or maritime comforts. They were strictly into the business of shark-fishing, and their attentions were riveted to the horizon and to the swells containing the occasional flashing gray, silvery streamlined forms of the quarry.

As he expected, Enda was put in charge of the surveillance drones and spent his time replenishing the bait tanks and checking the electronics. On one trip, he caught hell from Herman when one of his drones hit the water and was attacked by a bull shark, attracted to the spilling bait tank. The radar went blank, but the crew eventually retrieved the drone, and Enda was able to repair the damage.

One of the Arabs, a small man named Buca, admired how Enda handled himself during this episode and secretly offered him a drink from a small flask of whiskey, something ostensibly forbidden in his group. Buca mentioned how it was easier for him to get his hands on lyminiol than good Irish whiskey, which he enjoyed when he was away from home.

By the time the boat returned to the marina that evening, Enda had made a valuable contact for resupply of his drug stocks. As it turned out, Buca and several "friends" had a sea drone route to Cork, which Enda could tap into using a code supplied by Buca. This was good news to Enda, since Henson was no longer on the scene, and his supplies were running out.

But the downside to this was waiting for Enda. Sabo stepped from the shadows as Enda crossed the marina.

"You're a tough man to get hold of, Enda. I was beginning to think one of those sharks made a meal of you."

"They'd spit me right out," said Enda. "What are you doing here? I thought you'd be looking for Henson."

"Old Meaty has pulled up stakes and disappeared, probably left for greener pastures," said Sabo. "We won't be seeing him again. No matter, though, as I got my own source of supply. What I need are safe storage locations."

"I've got nothing that's safe, Sabo," said Enda. "The Gardai is watching everything. They've shut me down."

Sabo pulled a wooden fid from his pocket and slapped it against the side of Enda's head. A wound opened, and blood streamed onto Enda's pullover. He fell on one knee, wincing in pain.

"You gobshite," said Sabo. "Henson told us you have a crypt. They're won't be any Gardai watching it now, and I think it would be perfect. Give me the key, and maybe I'll let you have a piece of the action."

Two of Sabo's cronies joined them on the dock, but hung back in the shadows of the building.

Enda did have the key in his kit but knew that if he gave it to Sabo, odds were high that he would become fish bait within minutes.

"Okay, Sabo, I don't have the key with me. I keep it in a safe-deposit box at the bank. I'll have to get it tomorrow when they're open."

Sabo cupped Enda's bloody chin in his meaty hand and pulled his face up and said, "That's nice, Enda. We'll have our truck in the area at one o'clock tomorrow. You be sure to meet us at the crypt with the key. I *know* you'll be on time."

When Enda arrived home, his mobile rang with a message from Ellen, his mother's nurse. His mother had passed in the night, and Enda collapsed on the stairs in irreconcilable grief. Of course, he knew this day was coming, and he knew it would hit him hard when it did. He managed to put the subject out of mind until the time for his visit to his mother, and with his increasing activity on the shark boats, those visits were less frequent. Now it hit him full force. He was truly alone; the only person who really cared about him was taken—gone.

Enda suddenly thought of funerals as something more than a platform for social connections. He didn't want to attend a funeral for his mother; though he knew he must. He would not be outside looking in but every bit enmeshed in the pain of it from the inside. He had no friends or relatives who would offer him comfort, but he knew there were those who would try, just as he had at funerals he attended. There would be the brief, obligatory words, followed by much conversation among the guests, catching up on events since their last meeting, probably at another funeral. Life and pain must go on. He called Ellen to discuss the arrangements for his mother.

The bleeding had stopped, but his face was still hurting. Enda knew what he had to do. He fished up Garda Flaherty's number and dialed it on his bloodstained mobile.

"I have something of interest to tell you, Garda, something of mutual interest, as they say."

Enda arranged to meet Brenda Flaherty at his favorite pub. While he was never above getting a handout or a freebie himself, he was seldom one to make an offer. Certainly, the last group of people on earth he would favor with a compliment or a gratuity was the police. Nevertheless, he saw the Gardai now as a solution to a problem, and he offered to buy Brenda dinner, surprising himself in the process.

Brenda declined his offer but was anxious to have a meeting.

"Sit tight, McDonough. If you don't mind, I'm bringing along an old friend of yours, Garda Brannigan."

"In that case, you can buy me a drink and set a good example for Brannigan," Enda said.

Seated at a back table in the pub, Enda had his head wrapped in a makeshift bandage. He was savoring an ale when Brenda and Brannigan walked in, and he presumptuously ordered two more.

"What the hell happened to you?" Brannigan said. "Did you get in a fight on the shark boat?"

Enda was silent.

"I sense you have something good to tell us," Brenda teased. "Just so we're clear. I've got nothing on you if I like what you're going to say."

"Like I told you before, I have no drugs," Enda lied. "But here's the thing. I can tell you where you can put your hands on Sabo's stash, or at least some of it, and get him and his goons in the process."

"I can see the bastard made another enemy," Brenda said. "I'm all ears."

She took a swig of ale, more enthusiastically now.

Following Enda's disclosure about the upcoming meeting at the crypt, Brenda excused herself and went to the ladies' room. She made two calls on her mobile: first, to Sergeant Pat Twomey to line up reinforcements; second, to Declan McGuinness.

"As far as Enda McDonough is concerned, Sabo burned all his bridges. I think the hatred is real and visceral. We'll get him now, Inspector."

"Bring HCLs, Brenda, but if at all possible, we want to take this guy alive," Declan said with excitement in his voice. "I'll be in Kinsale tomorrow morning.

Early the following day, Twomey and Brannigan dispatched a whisper drone to hover high above the site of the crypt and send back video images to the station. The drone was undetectable with the sun behind it, and the motors virtually silent.

Around half past noon, a white biofuel van was detected, crawling along the cemetery road toward Enda's crypt. Twomey alerted Brenda and the drug squad officers lurking in the vicinity.

A red light flashed inside the van, accompanied by an audible blip. The drone was detected, and Sabo's driver attempted to turn the van around on the narrow road, almost overturning it. He gunned the engine, throwing up clouds of clay dust. The drone dropped in front of the van's windshield and shone a laser through the glass to the driver's chest while speeding backward ahead of the van. A booming voice warned the driver to stop while the maw of an HCL became apparent at the front of the drone. There was no escaping. The van screeched to a halt, and the doors fell open.

Sabo and his two accomplices were cuffed by Gardai and led to a waiting police bus. Brenda and Declan opened the rear doors of Sabo's van and found it stuffed with boxes of coffee pods. Examination disclosed they contained high quality lyminiol, probably manufactured in Libya, maybe even Con Mercer's facility.

Enda received a call from Brenda Flaherty late that afternoon to tell him that Sabo and two of his men had been arrested, thanking him for his cooperation. Enda breathed a sigh of relief and thought, now he could store his mother's ashes properly.

CHAPTER 34

The drug bust at St. Mary's cemetery made the local news, and Kinsale received the kind of notoriety the townies definitely did not want. The Kinsale Station referred all questions to the superintendent's public-relations office in Cork, and Brenda and Declan maintained their low profiles in the area. Declan did agree to an interview in Cork in the hope that he could send a message to Doug Henson (again assuming he was still alive) that he should turn himself in for a possible reduced sentence. He was able to link Henson to Sabo and even to the attempt to kill Brenda.

The superintendent was glad to learn that Bob Foley had hired Peter Collins to help track down the ransom payment. Since Collins was required to turn his findings over to the Gardai, Declan thought it somewhat shameful that the Gardai would reduce its operating budget at Bob's expense and earn unwarranted kudos from the press if Henson was caught.

Bob accepted the situation because he knew it would be easier now for the super to approve a trip to Libya for himself and Brenda. He had to confirm once and for all that Henson was dead or alive. He knew Ireland was a small part of the Republic of Europe, and even though kidnapping was a national offense, the politics of retrieving ransom placed his problem low in the queue with Brussels or the Interpol. Getting Henson was a different matter.

Peter Collins had a unique approach to solving the case. He took a page from Alex Osborn's 1941 management primer dealing with the technique, which came to be known as "brainstorming." He wanted to assemble a key group who would ostensibly have the most knowledge of Henson, ask them the same questions, and let their answers infuse into the most logical pattern. Unfortunately, many of the most knowledgeable persons would be dead, in prison, unavailable, or unwilling to participate. Collins knew that and decided he would take the product achieved by the principal group and individually play that against the input of persons—like Sabo—who would be separately interviewed. This was certainly imperfect, but it was interesting. Declan had seen Collins use the technique before and was impressed with the results he managed to obtain.

It was time for Collin's first meeting, and the group he assembled at Sham Rock could be counted on to have a largely negative view of Doug Henson. There was Bob and Jim Foley, of course, along with Declan McGuinness, Brenda Flaherty, and finally, some of the crew on approved leave of absence from the *Fancy Fran*. At the last minute, Enda McDonough reluctantly agreed to participate, being given little choice by Declan and Brenda.

Collins turned his recorder on and said, "I'm not interested in what you thought of Henson's morals or honesty. Tell me what you think about his favorite interests, likes, and dislikes. Were there certain kinds of persons he enjoyed spending time with. Did he ever indicate his plans for the future?"

Before long, Henson was clearly portrayed as a consummate loner with no real friends. He enjoyed the occasional company of women but had no romantic interest in anyone of any gender. He enjoyed life on the yacht and loved boating even though he was not much of a sailor. Bob Foley thought he had an unusual amount of interest in genealogy, in particular his own and Bob's origins. This could be explained by the fact that Henson was adopted, never knew his birth parents, and had a startling resemblance to Bob, or would have had his face not been damaged.

The FF crew members could not add anything to that but did say Henson was very sensitive on the subject of his scarred face. The sobriquet of "Meatface" was not to be used in his presence if one valued their skin. Henson wore no jewelry, not even a wristwatch, and liked to wear loose, informal clothing whenever he could—nothing unusual there. He had no tattoos and was normally clean-shaven; though it had to be difficult for him.

Following another two weeks of meetings with others, including the imprisoned Sabo, Collins summoned Bob, Declan, and Brenda to a meeting at the Gardai District office in Cork. He seemed pleased with his progress and was accompanied by one of the forensics finance gurus from his firm.

"I think we can confidentially tell you where Henson has spent, or would spend, some of his ill-gotten gains. We may even have a line on where he would go to spend his future days," Collins said.

"That's encouraging, Peter," Declan said. "If Henson is still around, and we can even get into his general vicinity, it shouldn't take long to find him. Who could forget his face?"

"That's the rub, Declan," Collins said. "We think Henson is keeping a low profile aboard a sixty-five-foot yacht which he bought in Le Havre. The very fact that his face is a dead giveaway further convinced us that he would hide out on a boat. He probably has a crew of one or two and doesn't venture out much, except maybe to visit plastic surgeons."

"Wow! But wait a minute," Bob said. "I thought that the first thing I would do if I were Henson would be to get a face transplant. I checked it out on the internet and found it would cost him about five hundred thousand euros. That wouldn't have been a big deal for a guy like Henson, so why wait til now?"

"I can't say for sure, of course, but I suspect it has a lot to do with the years of anti-rejection medication that he would have to take following the surgery," Collins said. "All indications are that you and Henson are clones of the same person. He must have figured that out too. If he took your face, it would present no rejection problem, and it would fit like a glove with the least amount of preparatory surgery."

"Wait," said Declan. "That would mean Bob's life is in danger. Do we really think Henson could do this—find a surgeon who is compromised enough to agree to remove Bob's face from his corpse?"

The question hung in the air, waiting for an answer that wasn't coming.

"I'm not a medical expert," said Collins. "I suppose it could be possible to remove someone's face without killing him and replace it with skin grown on a casting, but I don't think it would be very pleasant for Bob—assuming it were feasible.

"We're all speculating here, including about whether or not Henson is even still alive. How does anyone of us know that Henson wants to have plastic surgery?" Declan asked. "It may seem logical, but we don't know anything for sure."

"True enough, Dec," Bob said. "But since both Peter and I had the same thought about this, I sure want to watch my back, check my insurance policies, so to speak."

"Brenda and I have got your back, Bob," said Declan, turning to Peter Collins. "How do you know Henson bought a yacht?"

"We just followed the boat lead from our meetings and decided he would want a boat he could operate by himself or with a small crew. We didn't think he could handle it alone, so worked the most likely algorithm, came up with sixty to seventy feet." Collins then turned to his colleague.

"We checked all the European boatyards, looking for a new or retrofitted yacht sold within the past year to a man looking like Henson," the man sitting next to Collins said. "We got lucky and came up with this."

He handed Bob a picture of a small yacht, rechristened with the name *Graystone* painted across the stern.

"That's it," said Bob. "There couldn't be two boats with that name!"

He handed the picture of his birth father to Collins and showed him the writing on the back of the photo.

"What's home berth for this boat?" Brenda said.

"Libya, or more specifically, Benghazi," Collins said. "But he's not there now. According to Interpol, the boat went north, not sure where."

"Henson has strong drug ties in Libya," Brenda said. "Now he's got some seed money to start an operation of his own. Everything is fitting together. Nice work, Mr. Collins."

The meeting ended with some final words about confiscating the yacht and tracking Henson's account.

"We'll work on getting the remainder of your assets, Bob," said Collins. "Bringing Henson to justice is now in the hands of the Gardai."

"Perfect," said Declan. "But first things first. Garda Flaherty and I are going to Libya to check out a body."

CHAPTER 35

Declan, Brenda, and Bob left the meeting with Collins and headed to the English Market where they enjoyed lunch and the happy culmination to a long, frustrating week. Ideas were bubbling between Declan and Brenda about their forthcoming trip to Libya and where and how they would proceed if, as signs were pointing, Henson was alive. Bob was beaming in a self-satisfied glow; his decision to hire Peter Collins was a good one, and the payoff was within sight.

"I have to work a missing persons case, Bob," said Declan. "It looks fairly simple and shouldn't take much of my time. Brannigan and I can keep you in sight while I'm doing it, and I can work out of Kinsale. I think Peter is right. Henson will be coming for you because, as grotesque as it may sound, you've got something he wants. Brenda can go ahead of me to Benghazi, and I'll meet her at Mercer's office."

Brenda was anxious to get to Libya where she had an old contact. She decided the contact would have to wait for another time as she unpacked her kit suited for desert travel. As it turned out, she'd spend more time in Benghazi than in the desert, but she couldn't know it at the time. She wondered how Declan was going to identify the corpse, which the Libyan police assured her was still at Wolf's campsite at a cordoned location. No medical examination was performed, which seemed totally irregular to Brenda, but the police were shorthanded and told that an ME would be supplied by the FBI.

Brenda obtained a written report and a poor English translation. She could speak a little Arabic, picked up during her Special Forces days, and with the help of her digital translator, learned that the FBI had no intention of doing a medical examination unless the complete remains were transported to their lab in Benghazi. That wasn't happening, and the whole identification cock-up was hanging on an engraving on an HCL found near the body.

Declan arrived at the hotel a few days after Brenda. He showered, changed his clothes, and headed for the bar to meet Brenda.

"We have no choice, Brenda," he said, sipping a gin. "We'll have to trek to Wolf's camp and see the whole mess for ourselves. The ME will have to wait until we can move the remains to Benghazi, but we have to put this ID to bed before that happens."

"There is one slim possibility, Mac," Brenda said, pursing her lips, squinting and rubbing her neatly turned chin. "Maybe we can find a witness to confirm who it was that got burned up."

"Good luck with that," Declan said. "I think it's safe to say that anyone on the scene besides Henson would not be inclined to tell us the truth—one of Henson's flunkies or a Mercer employee. And speaking of Mercer, I've arranged a meeting with him. We should be able to get to his office in about an hour. Are you okay with that?"

Brenda's face reddened as she conjured doing some real physical damage to Mercer.

"I can constrain myself, Mac, difficult though it may be. I just wonder if he'll remember me from our first meeting on the yacht. The son of a bitch looked me over like I was a piece of meat, most of the time staring at my chest and my rear end."

The offices of Mercer Enterprises were ensconced in a sleek glass building not far from the Mediterranean waterfront. From his upper story, he had a grand view of the coast, the docks, and of course, the *Fancy Fran*, resting at anchor in the afternoon sunlight. Brenda's hunch turned out to be correct. When Mercer was introduced, he didn't remember her but did spent minutes perusing the lines of her figure, as revealed beneath her well-fitted Gardai uniform, which she wore for the occasion.

"It's sad that Doug Henson was killed in the desert," Mercer said after his guests settled into chairs and sipped his offering of tea. "He was a severe disappointment, though, and we have no idea what he may have done with the ransom he got from Jim Foley's father."

"I'm curious, Mr. Mercer," Declan said. "How was Henson able to get so quickly from the Ritz Amaz Hotel in Benghazi to Wolf's desert camp, and why do you think he would go back to the camp?"

"He never contacted me after he rescued Dr. Foley, Inspector," Mercer said. "He may have thought that Wolf returned to his camp after he escaped from the hotel. You must realize that after Henson rescued Jim Foley, and I learned of his bank transfer, my former chief of security became persona non grata to me."

"I find it hard to believe that Henson would care about where Wolf would go once he rescued Jim Foley and had the ransom money," Declan said. "Tell you what I think. Henson wasn't burned up in the desert, and that body belongs to someone else. We'll find out soon enough."

Declan studied Mercer's face for any sign of reaction to his words, but the magnate was as impassive as stone.

Mercer had Declan and Brenda flown to his desert site on one of his drones. After they arrived and surveyed the damage, they interviewed some of the personnel left behind and learned of Sadiq's trip to find Wolf's camp and Jim Foley. Declan was disappointed to find that none of the workers went with Sadiq, so he didn't have a witness to any of the events at Wolf's camp. He did find, however, that Henson subsequently arrived at the Mercer site then left with two of his men to follow Sadiq to Wolf's camp. It became clear which direction he and Brenda would have to go to get to the camp.

Brenda learned that the drone returning from Wolf's camp brought two women who were later put to work in the Mercer mess. Three men returned from the camp with the women, but it was at night, and the lighting was minimal. The workers couldn't determine whether or not one of the men was Henson, or so they said. But maybe now Brenda had her witness. One of the women agreed to travel with her and Declan to Wolf's camp.

The wreckage at Wolf's camp turned out to be of little worth in shedding light on what had occurred there. There wasn't much left of the body in the burned-out drone rubble. Declan was glad he wouldn't have to listen to complaints from an ME about the condition of the body or the crime scene.

179

The young woman they brought with them seemed to be more comfortable in Brenda's company and was soon talking freely. With her digital translator, Brenda was able to determine that "the tall man with the scarred face had blackened a pistol and thrown it on the ashes near the body." Bingo!

Declan, Brenda, and the woman went back to the drone to prepare for the trip back to Mercer's site. Declan finished taking some photos of the scene then turned to Brenda with a satisfied and determined expression.

"Okay, let's consider where we are." As he looked at Brenda, he was reminded of their nearly fatal trip out to Mercer's yacht. On that occasion, she wore body armor which saved her life. "Now we know Henson left the desert alive, rescued Jim Foley, grabbed the ransom, and made good his escape. No more wondering about that. And just by process of elimination, I think the burned body belongs to this guy Sadiq."

"I agree, Mac," said Brenda. "Sadiq was not at Mercer's site nor Wolf's camp. That means he either left with Henson and his boys or the only body found at the camp is his. The Mercer crew told me Sadiq had a bad laser wound, and I can empathize with that. I can't see Henson taking him to Benghazi. He wouldn't give a damn about Sadiq and would consider him unnecessary baggage."

"The body might belong to one of Wolf's crew, but I don't think so. The woman would have told you that," said Declan. "The Libyans should be able to confirm the identity by checking Mercer's employment records. I think we can finish up here and get back."

After Declan returned to the hotel in Benghazi, he decided to check in with Cork and bring his super up-to-date. Though absent a medical examiner's report, the superintendent decided to accept Declan's conclusion that Henson was alive, and the search for this criminal and alleged murderer needed to continue. He was agreeable to letting Brenda Flaherty continue on the case, subject to Declan's oversight. Declan was doubly glad for this determination; he wouldn't have to tell Brenda that she couldn't nail the adversary who tried to kill her, and also, he wouldn't lose a very capable partner.

Declan had a difficult decision to make. He wanted to return to Kinsale to make sure his friend, Bob Foley, was safe. Brannigan couldn't cover Bob round the clock, and there wasn't enough manpower at the Kinsale post to do it. At the same time, he was afraid Brenda might get into difficulty going after Henson by herself. Was splitting up a good idea? he wondered. Eventually, he decided, based on all intelligence so far, Henson should be making his way to Kinsale to get Bob, and Brenda would be right behind. It was better for Henson to be outflanked in this way. Besides, Brenda was well able and motivated. With Declan to the north, and Brenda to the south, the pincer movement would be in play.

Declan was not about to spend the next few days in Kinsale, sipping Bob's Jameson whiskey, much as that image seemed appealing to him. Brenda did indicate she had a close police contact in Benghazi who could help her with the tracking, and that could be crucial to success. In addition, if Brenda was going to be risking another laser dogfight, she would be in a better position if Declan could communicate Henson's whereabouts as precisely as possible. There seemed to be a way to do this.

CHAPTER 36

Interpol had perfected a satellite surveillance system with the aid of the United States, known as the automatic identification system (AIS). Boats as large as Henson's *Graystone* would be required to have an installed radio beacon, which would project a unique signature. Even if the beacon were disabled, the boat could still be tracked, and the absence of the beacon would be a signal for the coast guard to investigate. The AIS, originally developed to zero in on illegal fishing, was now contributing to safety and crime prevention on a variety of fronts. Declan's laptop showed a scan of the Atlantic and various coastlines which enabled him, with the help of Interpol, to track any large vessel making its way toward the Bandon River.

Brenda Flaherty was also engaged in a proactive plan of her own. She would be attempting to track the whereabouts of Henson from Libya. Brenda had a contact in Libya, going back to her days in Special Forces.

Samidra Abizaid (Sami) was born in Bronx, New York, and emigrated to Libya when she was a teenager. She stayed in Libya to help her ailing parents whose home was overrun by a rebel group. Following the death of her parents, she joined the new Libyan Security Force and traveled back to the United States and to England for additional training, eventually rising to the rank of lieutenant.

Sami and Brenda met in the Middle East while on assignment with the UN. They became fast friends, especially after Brenda's husband was killed, and Brenda had seemingly nowhere to turn.

Brenda contacted Sami through official channels, and they greeted one another warmly at the airport in Benghazi. Brenda wasted no time in bringing Sami up to speed on the case and asked for her assistance. Since Sami was on leave and between jobs and romances, she was very glad for the diversion. Also, Sami's office was happy to cooperate.

Sitting in the airport restaurant, Sami and Brenda passed Brenda's case file back and forth, highlighting and commenting on various portions and sipping hot tea.

"Tell me something, Brenda," Sami said. "Aren't clones like identical twins? How could one confiscate the face of the other? Twins wouldn't do that. This private detective must be wrong."

"They're not brothers," Brenda said. "They have no relationship other than DNA, didn't know of each other's existence til months ago. They're physically the same, I suppose, but their mental wiring is completely different. One is a clean-living, loving parent, the other a sociopath. My own thoughts are that twins might never do this, but how much experience does society have with human clones?"

"Okay, but I'm thinking no plastic surgeon with the gravitas to do this job would touch it if they knew Bob Foley was murdered to provide the face."

Sami crossed her shapely, dark-toned legs and asked a waitress in Arabic to bring them some English biscuits.

"I agree, Sami," Brenda said. "That means we have to find some shady, underworld plastic surgeon who can remove Bob's face, pack it in a container with nitrogen, and make it appear that it's coming from a legitimate donor organization. But would this surgeon have to be in Libya?"

"He could be anywhere in the world," Sami said. "As long as the transport time for the container with the face is within the limits required for viability."

"And what is that?" said Brenda. She made a mental note that she would have to research this medical topic.

"Damned if I know."

Sami said they would be better off finding the marina where Henson berthed his boat and to interrogate the owner. Brenda agreed and the two left in Sami's BMW robo.

Sami's office located the marina after a few phone calls and relayed the information to her as she headed for the waterfront. She was also able to reserve a sea drone armed with HCLs in the event they might be needed. Brenda rubbed her arm as she remembered the searing blast of the laser over Bandon River. She told Sami to keep a safe distance if they did go out after Henson and spot his boat and to make sure she was wearing her laser-proof vest.

The marina turned out to be a private facility at the shore end of a long pier. A guard was standing at an entrance gate, and he waved the BMW to a stop. The guard smiled when he saw Sami's ID and explained that the *Graystone* departed two weeks prior, no itinerary or return date given; four men on board. The guard's log listed four names: D. Graystone, S. McCarthy, B. Kahn, and J. Namibi, MD.

"Tell me about the doctor," Brenda said as she jotted down the name.

Sami was on her mobile, checking with her office.

"He was short, had a rumpled suit, and brought a lot of equipment, it seemed, including a cart and several tanks of liquid or gas," the guard said. "We helped him get it all onboard."

Sami turned to Brenda and said, "Namibi has a history. He was suspended from medical practice for two years when he was named as a target in a pedophile case. He was found guilty of treating and not reporting HCL wounds, lost his license for that one. Big file, my office says, but nothing that would put him in jail."

Brenda called Declan McGuinness.

"We think Henson is heading to Kinsale to nab Bob Foley. He has a doctor of nefarious reputation on board, and we think he plans to make Bob an unwitting face donor for his future surgery. Has Interpol or the coast guard located the *Graystone* yet?"

"Yeah, they put in at the Port of Brest in Western Brittany, France," Declan said. "He's too far away for you to get to by drone. See if you can get a charter to Brest at Interpol's expense. I'll make some calls from my end."

"How is Bob Foley holding up?" Brenda said. "He should probably head for Cork and spend time with his girlfriend. That's got to be better than waiting for Henson at Sham Rock."

"He won't do it, Brenda," Declan said. "Unfortunately, I'll have to go to Cork for a few days myself. Something's come up on my missing-person case. A body was found. Brannigan's been assigned to keep watch at the Rock, and Daly can spell him when needs be. Sergeant Twomey will track the *Graystone* while I'm gone."

Brenda and Sami barely left the dock when the guard fiddled with his mobile, raising it to his ear.

"Two cops were looking for you, Mr. Henson. I think they probably figured out where you went."

"No problem, Gus," said Henson. "We'll be prepared for a nice, little chat."

Brenda said a sad goodbye to Sami at the airport, "You'll probably be married with kids by the next time I see you."

"Don't count on it, Bren," Sami said. "Guys head the other way when they find out what I do for a living. I don't care. When I retire, I want to find a rich widower with a lovely family, preferably a daughter who loved her mother and a son who challenges his father every day. And I don't want ever to clone myself. When I go, the mold goes with me. Devil take it all."

The Interpol arranged an EDF surveillance aircraft for Brenda, and she was treated to a meal of sandwiches and beer when they reached altitude. She was permitted to carry an HCL pistol but hoped she wouldn't have to use it. She much preferred a meeting with Henson in which she had the opportunity to smash his smug, scarred face with her gloved fist. Foolish thinking, she realized. As far as it was possible, her takedown of him would have to be clinical and unemotional. To survive, she would have to get the first shot. Henson would be no pushover.

Brest came into view as the plane wheeled for a landing. It was as beautiful and inviting a port as ever you'd want. The Tour Tanguy and the Chapeau de Brest could be seen through a pale overcast, reminders that successful defense works in their day only had to withstand lightly lobbed cannonballs. Now they were carefully preserved tourist attractions.

Brenda referred to her file and carefully memorized the lines of the *Graystone*. She hoped to spot the boat from the air but knew her chances were slim to none. From the plane's altitude, Henson's boat would be too small to have much definition. Nevertheless, she marked a few likely candidates on the map of the coast she had spread on her lap. She hoped that a drone would be available for a closer, more-detailed search. She hoped the Interpol would be accommodating after she landed.

She called Sergeant Twomey to determine if he had the *Graystone* on his screen. He provided the coordinates which Brenda checked on her map. They matched one of the locations she marked.

It was getting late, so Brenda booked into a small hotel near the waterfront. She was unpacking her gear when her mobile rang. She was expecting a call from Interpol but was pleasantly surprised even though it wasn't Interpol on the call.

"Guess what, Bren?" Sami said on the other end. "You're not getting rid of me after all. My boss nearly wet his pants when I told him you were in Brest, chasing Henson. He wants me to hook up with you and join the hunt."

Brenda was only slightly surprised when Sami said that Libyan Intelligence and Interpol suspected that a shipment of cocaine was being delivered to Brest. The fact that Henson had holed up in Brest couldn't have been a coincidence.

"Why not, Sami?" Brenda said. "Henson has the money and the means. He's probably looking for a new enterprise now that he's parted company with Mercer."

Brenda decided she had better call Declan and bring him up-to-date.

"You and your Libyan friend will need backup," Declan told her. "Sounds like Henson may be expanding. Ask Interpol to tap the French for support. Everybody likes to get in on a drug bust."

CHAPTER 37

After Brenda picked up Sami at the airport, Interpol kept their promise and delivered a drone. It was a small EDF craft with floats, and Brenda was eventually able to land close to the pier, which matched the coordinates provided by Twomey. The *Graystone* was nowhere to be seen. Unfortunately, she landed close enough to be spotted by one of Henson's goons, who was hiding behind a bait shack, scanning the pier with binoculars. He wasted no time contacting Henson.

Brenda called Interpol so they could help in arranging backup. She was pocketing her mobile when she saw the glint of binoculars on the pier. Sami had taken control of the drone.

"Take it up, Sami," said Brenda. "Let's see if we can spot the *Graystone* before any backup arrives. Safe to say Henson will know we're here now."

Aboard the *Graystone*, Henson was adjusting the focus of his binoculars. He was scanning the horizon when the alert came that Brenda and Sami arrived at the pier.

"Those two squat cops got here faster than I thought they would," he said to his crewmate. "They don't know where we are now, but they'll have backup coming soon, and the entire coast will be scoured. Time for our little surprise."

The four motors purred with their shimmering, spinning, twisting propellers, carrying the drone hundreds of meters straight up into the coastal air, now hovering in the downdraft which had quickly dried the pontoons.

"Where we going, Bren?" Sami said. "What's the plan?"

"Take it north slowly then south along the coast. Keep a sharp lookout for anything that looks like Henson's boat. I'm going to try calling Sergeant Twomey to see if he can pick anything up on his scanner," Brenda said.

She knew the drone could be a target for Henson, who surely knew of their presence by this time. She shuddered at the painful memory of the laser hitting her arm when she and Declan flew out to meet the *Fancy Fran* in Kinsale. The scar from that episode would be a lifelong reminder of that encounter.

"Keep the control on manual, Sami. If we see *any* boat, you'll need to take the drone down fast to a few feet above the water."

Twomey came back on the mobile, saying, "I lost Henson's boat. He must have disengaged the AIS tracker. Why wouldn't he? He has bigger things to worry about than the coast guard at this point. But something else came up." Twomey savored the moment, as it wasn't often he could participate in an adventure of this magnitude from the confines of his Kinsale office. "The screen shows a large blip about two nautical miles from your coordinates. The registry code shows it to be a garbage scow from Portugal."

"What's a garbage scow doing way up here in tourist territory?" Brenda said. "We're going to check it out, Sarge."

Brenda had no time to sign off with Twomey when a whooshing sound and an earsplitting crash left a smoking hole through the starboard pontoon. Familiar images flashed in Brenda's brain. Sami instinctively brought the drone down to within a few meters above the water, trailing smoke from the pontoon as she descended.

"What the hell was that?" gushed Sami, who moments before had been watching the sea, which appeared as a tranquil sheet of tiny, glinting specks from their lofty height. Now the ocean turned ominous, and the specks had grown to crowding fists with foam fingers reaching for them.

"That was a heavy-duty laser, but it didn't come from the scow," Brenda said. "They may still be able to target us down here, but it will be more difficult. I'm going to land on the scow so we can check the damage. There should be plenty of room for us."

As they approached the scow, the mountain of garbage loomed large, filling most of the cargo space and wearing a crown of circling gulls. The fetid odor wafted downwind, so Brenda decided to land on top from the other side. There was no one in sight.

"Shit," said Sami. "I just had my hair done last week. I'll never get that smell out."

"You're going to get a lot messier, Sami. I need you to check out that pontoon and anything else that may have been hit. You're the amateur mechanic, not me."

After Sami got to work, Brenda scanned the distant pilothouse at the fore end of the scow and spotted a bulky seaman carrying an HCL, heading their way. She decided to take the chance that the man would be more curious than aggressive, and waved both her arms and walked toward him. This worked for a while, but the man raised his weapon and fired, burning into Brenda's body armor.

The seaman's laser was not set on full power, but Brenda's HCL was. He crumbled and fell dead, just as another man exited the pilothouse with his arms raised. He wasn't carrying a weapon but from his cap looked like he might be the vessel's skipper.

"C'mon, Sami. Let's check this out," Brenda called back.

Sami stepped to the cargo walkway, a rancid mess, obviously thinking this was not what she bargained for.

With the help of her translator app, Brenda determined that the scow skipper was paid to deliver a shipment of drugs to Brest. His family was threatened, he claimed, and a goon was sent with him as insurance. Brenda and Sami had no reason not to believe him, especially since he quickly showed them where the stash was hidden on the vessel. The quantity of drugs turned out to be even larger than Interpol intelligence reported earlier: hundreds of kilos of heroine, lyminiol, and cocaine, professionally packaged and stowed beneath the pilothouse, millions of euros in street value. Sami's superiors would definitely be ecstatic. This would trump all the reward promises they reneged on in the past. To make sure she would get her due, she had her picture taken standing beside the drugs with the captain and Brenda.

Brenda called the coast guard and provided information on the haul, along with identification details for the captain and the dead guard. They said they were already on their way to the area to investigate the lost AIS signal from the *Graystone*. From the last position sent, Henson would have gone north from Brest, taking him farther from a rendezvous with the scow. According to the captain, Henson was given coordinates for the scow. Brenda wondered why then would Henson go in the opposite direction. Perhaps he wanted to throw the coast guard off before turning south to get the drugs.

"No," Brenda said aloud, more to herself. "With the AIS turned off, Henson thinks the coast guard won't find him. He's not worried about them. If he wanted the drugs, he would have headed straight for the scow."

"Wait," Sami said, puzzled by Brenda's disconnected thought. "Aren't the drugs why your boy came to Brest?"

"Sure," said Brenda. "But what about that plastic surgeon he's got on board? What's he going to do with the drugs? He has no distribution network. We don't know what Henson's feckin' agenda is. He's in no hurry to pick up these drugs because he has them well-disguised in a pile of garbage."

"And he doesn't know we're here," interjected Sami. "He probably thinks we're out there swimming with the fishes, and his stash is safe."

"If you're right, Sami, time is on our side," said Brenda. "But if you're wrong, the coast guard will never get here before he does, and we'll both have to hide out in the garbage."

Sami didn't like the idea of losing what she considered *her* drug bust.

"I'm willing to take my chances, Bren. I'll sit on the drugs until the coast guard arrives, and you can fly back to Brest. The drone will make it. The damaged pontoon has several watertight compartments, but only one is holed. When you land, it will fill with water, and you'll probably taxi in circles, but you won't sink."

Brenda looked sadly at her friend. They both knew if Henson was heading for the scow, they would probably be seeing each other for the last time.

"Well, you can't go back to France smelling like you do." Brenda hugged Sami, becoming aware for the first time that her body armor had been burned through more than halfway. "One thing I always

190

wanted to tell you, Sami," Brenda said, "you really stink!" They both laughed.

Brenda tried to call Declan McGuinness on the vessel's radio but was unable to make a connection. Her call was directed to Sergeant Twomey's mobile.

"He's on his way to Brest," Twomey said. "He's in the air and probably has his mobile turned off. He said he was going to contact you straight away when he got in. He's up-to-date on all events, so to speak."

"Except he doesn't know yet that I killed a man on the garbage scow and ruined a brand-new armor vest in the process," Brenda said.

"Garda Brenda Flaherty," Twomey huffed. "You're going to need to talk to a counselor when you get back, regulations, you know."

"I'll set it up when I get back to Belfast," Brenda lied. "Meantime, I'll hang my vest up as a reminder of how close I came to joining the spirits in the bog. That should suppress any feelings of guilt."

Brenda flew the drone back toward Brest, barely skimming the wave tops. She didn't know for sure if the laser that hit the drone came from Henson's boat but was fairly certain it must have. At this range from shore, even a heavy-duty laser blast would have dissipated over the Atlantic before damaging the drone. Unfortunately, as Brenda came closer to the Brest coast, she couldn't keep the low profile she hoped for. The twisted metal around the hole in the pontoon was resonating in the rushing air, emitting a loud, unpleasant, whistling whine. She didn't notice this before; something had changed, perhaps the wind velocity. Reducing speed helped, but there was no way now she could be stealthy. She was carrying a pipe organ on the starboard side and was not enthralled with this newfound musical addition.

Back in Brest, Declan called Brenda, "What's that whistle?"

CHAPTER 38

Brenda detailed her situation to Declan after exclaiming how glad she was to finally be hearing from him.

Declan said, "I know your friend is staying with the drugs on that garbage scow, but it wasn't a good idea to split up. Henson is going to be even more of a threat now he knows you're close on his heels. Do you have enough electric charge to make it to Brest?"

"Yeah," said Brenda. "The solar rechargers are working full-time. Laser didn't touch them. I'm not going to Brest, though, because Henson isn't there. I'm going north up the coast to an anchorage I saw on the charts. We can meet up there."

"Good call," Declan said. "Henson wanted out of Brest because he knew the authorities would be there once he learned you were in the area. Also, he knew coast-guard drones would be searching the Atlantic near the coast. The anchorage would make a good hiding place for the time being. I was told about the anchorage by the French police. Incidentally, in case you were wondering, the French and the Libyans split up when they heard about the garbage scow. Half went with the coast guard to be in on the drug seizure. It's amazing how many want their pictures on the internet next to that pile of goodies."

"What about the other half, Mac?" Brenda asked.

She now found she could change the note of the whistle by altering the speed of the drone.

"About five others are going up the coast to the anchorage. We'll meet you up there. No time for lunch. We'll leave right away."

"What the hell is that noise?" barked Henson, aboard the *Graystone*, adjusting the focus of his glasses. "Sounds like a banshee in labor." He squinted, accentuating the scars in his face. "It's that

Gardai bitch again, nine lives like a feckin' cat. How the hell did she find me? I shut off the AIS."

"I can pop her from here, Boss," the crewman said. "Just say the word."

"No," Henson said. "We don't know who she's with. We don't want to attract attention. Call Frenchy and postpone our meeting."

He turned toward the wheelhouse and shouted to the pilot to get underway.

"Too late, Boss," the crewman said. "Two boats have come in after us and dropped anchor. We're not getting out of here anytime soon."

"They have nothing on you guys or the doctor," Henson said. "It's me they want." There was a tower near the anchorage, similar but smaller than the Tanguy. A tourist agency owned a four-passenger drone, which operated from a helipad on top of the tower. "I'll slip off in the small boat, make it to the tower, and blend in with the tourists. I'll meet with you later up the coast. Send me your coordinates."

Brenda knew she was spotted and cursed her luck and the whistling pontoon. In the commotion on the *Graystone*, she saw the small boat push away from the *Graystone* and suspected it was Henson. She took the drone to the top of the tower and landed on the heliport. There was a small office to the side, unoccupied at the moment. A window in the office looked out on the scene hundreds of meters below. A long rope connected to the high window was used for adjusting the opening. Standing at the lower window, Brenda could see the *Graystone* being boarded by the French police and Interpol. She used a scope she took from the drone and scanned the crowd along the pier. She saw no one or anything suspicious.

Henson had seen Brenda fly the drone to the top of the tower and instantly formed an escape plan. There was a lift in the tower which went all the way to the top. If he ascended to the heliport, he could kill Brenda and fly her drone out. He was alone on the lift as he rode up but nevertheless gripped the HCL pistol hidden under his jacket.

The lift door opened to the heliport office, and he spotted Brenda, looking out the window with her back turned to him. He was about to pull the trigger on his HCL when he suddenly had a different idea.

"Turn around and face me with your hands raised, bitch. You wanted to find me so bad, so here I am. I tried three times to have you frazzled, but you got lucky. Guess what? Your luck just ran out, and your drone is just sitting there waiting for me."

"How far do you think you're going to get, Henson? If you kill me and take that drone, they'll shoot you down in minutes. No questions asked."

Brenda was sure Henson would make good on his threat to become a cop killer this time.

"That's why you're going with me, Delaney, or whatever your name is."

Henson slammed her with the butt of his pistol and pushed her to the floor. He pulled down the window rope, cut off a length with his laser, and tied her hands behind her back.

Brenda was groggy and bleeding but able to get to her feet. The lift door opened, and a guard who had come to investigate the drone landing stepped out. Henson fired a low-level blast and hit the guard in the side. The guard doubled up in pain amid the smell of burning flesh and clothing.

"Tell them I've got the girl," Henson said in French with his voice lowered and deliberate.

The guard nodded, crouching in pain.

Declan, arriving with the French police, had also seen Brenda land on top of the tower but didn't see Henson. He made his way to the lift, pushed the button, and waited for it to descend to ground level. When he heard the unique fizzle of an HCL being discharged somewhere above, he decided he couldn't wait for the lift and rushed to the stairway door. This turned out to be a mistake. The seldom-used stairs were narrow, with overly long risers. The staircase was circular, claustrophobic, and dank, a medieval torture space obviously not built or modified to modern European building or safety standards. Declan tired quickly and, with heart-pounding effort, decided to return to the lift. When he finally arrived at the top of the tower and received Henson's message from the wounded guard, he was able to see the drone whirling away in the distance as the sound of the whistling pontoon faded. Declan knew Brenda was on the drone, so he assumed that she must still be alive—Henson's hostage. He was terribly saddened that he had failed her, experiencing one of the lowest points in his life.

Henson guessed his boat would be seized and that, at least for a while, he would be safer traveling anonymously on a charter. He set a course north to fly the drone low and close to the coastline. He hoped he could get to a charging station before the power ran too low. He put the drone into manual control and turned out to sea. When he thought he was over deep enough water, his plan was to toss Brenda out and then head back on course up the coast. He would ensure he was out of sight of all prying eyes, and the police would assume Brenda was still onboard and give him safe passage. When he got to the desired location, he opened the portside door, which rose like a clamshell.

Unfortunately for Henson, his knot-tying skills had not improved since he tied the anchor to Scarlet Kelly's foot many months ago. Brenda was able to wriggle out of her bonds with very slight motion while also feigning semiconsciousness as a result of her wounded head. Perspiration rolled down her fingers as she reached ever so slowly for the combat throwing knife in her boot side pocket. Henson was busy putting the drone into hover mode and removing his seatbelt. He was not aware of Brenda's lightning strike until the arterial blood was spurting from his neck. The sudden loss of blood pressure brought loss of consciousness, and he fell forward onto the control panel. The entire aircraft rolled, and Henson slipped off his seat and out the open door. He hurdled a thousand meters to the ocean below.

Brenda slid across the floor of the drone before she could get to the controls. Henson's blood made it difficult for her to get purchase, and she slipped out the door, managing to snag the hole in the pontoon at the last second. Two of the drone's motors started to whine from the strain of trying to keep the craft from turning completely over. Brenda's grip was tenuous, and the pain in her hand substantial as the drone started a slow descent toward the ocean.

Brenda's Special Forces training came to the fore, and with prodigious effort, she managed to pull herself back inside the pod. Within seconds she righted the drone and turned it back on a heading to the anchorage. Now fully automatic, the drone could fly itself, and Brenda collapsed in the seat with her head in her hands. Her mouth was dry, and if there was supposed to be any sweetness in revenge, it completely escaped her. Surprisingly, the whistling noise stopped; her grip on the pontoon had crimped some of the loose metal, removing its ability to act as a reed. She cried softly for several minutes and then called Declan to tell him she was coming in—alone.

Declan's relief was palpable, and his voice quaked as he told her what a great job she had done. Then silently Declan realized what he said was pedestrian, insufficient, stupid. It was the inspector and superior speaking, and he wished he could take it back. Now he could only picture his friend and colleague sitting next to him high over the Bandon River, with her precious life draining down her arm. She wasn't much older than his own daughter, but there was no one he felt closer to at this moment and no one he was happier to see or hear when she put down near the anchorage, even if she did smell slightly of garbage.

The *Graystone* was confiscated by the ER, along with hundreds of kilos of lyminiol found onboard. The crew and the doctor were held for questioning, and all were eventually charged.

The doctor said he didn't know who would be performing the surgery on Henson and tried to convince the prosecutor that he had no intention of killing Foley or removing his face. He claimed he didn't know who Bob Foley was, or when he would see him, but was only going to use Foley as a cellular model to grow a new face with 3D-printer technology. The prosecutor's medical expert doubted Dr. Namibi had the skills or equipment to do it. Besides, Namibi didn't have Bob Foley's permission and was unlikely to get it. Nevertheless, since the doctor didn't actually perform any illicit surgery, he was only charged with medical malpractice and lost his license for a second time.

Back at Sham Rock, Bob Foley got the news of Henson's death from Declan McGuinness. In his heart of hearts, Bob never fully accepted the idea that Henson wanted to "steal his face." Now, confronted with the facts vindicating Peter Collins's conclusions, he marveled at the paradox that nature could manufacture a "replica" with the audacity to be so different. Since Henson did rescue his son, however, he decided to light a candle for his fellow clone and set it on the mantel. He remembered an old saying that JJ taught him, "Even a good clock can give you the wrong time if it's wound too tight."

Peter Collins was eventually successful in getting most of Bob's stolen funds returned. Even after Peter's fee was deducted, the sum was substantial. Bob decided to establish a "Graystone Trust" for medical research. Otis Sham might not have approved, but Bob didn't care.

CHAPTER 39

The art promoter knew just what he wanted. He read the article about Sarah Benjamin and her Cork gallery in a reprint in the Australian magazine, *Art Front*. The article showed a picture of Sarah, an attractive, smiling, middle-aged woman standing next to a portrait in her gallery. The portrait caught his attention, and he was able to read a plate at the bottom of the frame with the aid of a magnifying glass: Graystone, Father of the Artist.

The article went on to say the portrait was painted by Sarah's soon-to-be fiancé named Bob, and an engagement party was going to take place in Kinsale. Nothing else referred to Bob as the piece dealt mainly with Sarah Benjamin's electronic system for displaying the works of new artists at subscribing institutions.

He decided he had to visit Sarah's gallery in Cork, see the system for himself, and check out the artist Bob. His company in Sydney would help with expenses, but the only available time window for the trip would conflict with Sarah and Bob's planned engagement party.

He e-mailed Sarah and confirmed the dates. Sarah had no objection to meeting him in Kinsale but added that she and Bob planned a trip to Spain after the engagement party. Sarah said she would provide the names and addresses for some institutional contacts in Cork with whom he could follow up. She attached a gallery brochure to her e-mail, and the promoter sent a link to his company's website.

It was a beautiful sunlit day in June when the robo bus rounded the corner near the tourist office and lumbered toward the stop opposite the newly renovated Upton Hotel. The festive air around the hotel indicated some kind of special event was underway. Strains of music and snippets of laughter drifted out from the well-appointed lobby.

The promoter was carrying his rolled-up copy of *Art Front* as he stepped from the bus and circled around to pick up his travel bag from the storage compartment. He walked over to the boat basin to look at the various watercraft. It was low tide, so all he saw were dank, fishy-smelling mud and a few decrepit, waterlogged dinghies. He smiled, as if familiar with the scene, then turned and walked toward the Upton.

Declan McGuinness was smiling as he walked out of the party room, glowing in an aura of incipient inebriation. His collar was open, and his tie hung limply and slightly spotted with cream sauce and Murphy's ale. He headed for the bar and ordered a Bushmills and soda. Behind and above the bartender a banner stretched across the wall: "Congratulations on your engagements—Bob and Sarah—Jim and Caitlin."

Declan turned with the drink in his hand then dropped it. He stared at the man with the rolled-up magazine, squinted, and rubbed his eyes.

"Jayzus, Mary, and Joseph. You can't be Bob. I just left you in the party room." Then a spark of realization came to him. "Of course! Shamrocks always count to three: one, two, three; red, yellow, blue; ready, set, go; Father, Son, Holy Spirit. Three is magical." He smiled broadly. "Why not three?"

The promoter was puzzled, put down his bag, and asked in a distinctly Australian accent, "Excuse me. I've been waiting for this moment since I was a child. Could you take me to Bob Graystone?"

The End

AFTERWORD

I t may seem overly optimistic that the devastations of climate change could be abated so quickly. Positive global changes by any reasonable estimate will surely take their time. Still, the opposite end point of letting the situation worsen is too depressing to contemplate. It's probable that many solutions to controlling greenhouse-gas emissions, all working together, will emerge over time, spurred on by visions of a dystopian future. Self-healing can only occur if we stop inflicting pain and address the wounds already made to the planet. There's no reason to believe this won't happen on a gradually increasing curve.

It also seems likely that there will be those like Conrad Mercer, who will take advantage of climate change in one way or another if there is financial gain to be had. Finding the bright side of the bad penny of climate change might be difficult, but to men like Mercer, it would be a challenge.

And what about cloning? Will human beings really be cloned in the future? The technology to do this already exists, as evidenced by the cloning of polo ponies in Argentina. Why anyone would want to clone a human, however, is debatable; but it seems that if it can be done, someone somewhere will eventually do it. And wouldn't that be a tricky round of events for bodies that might turn up in the future?

About the Author

Tom Cadogan is a retired engineer with a lifelong interest in the process of problem-solving. When he was a boy, growing up in New York City, his Irish-American parents used to scrounge the local library every week, looking for the latest mystery novel. It was inevitable that he should arrive at the writing of fiction after years of collecting data, finding problems, and searching for solutions. Eventually, he would need a place to share the creative combination of many recollections. The rebuilding of his heritage home in Ireland with his wife and brother would provide the platform for his first novel and infuse it with some memorable characters and experiences. His dream is that his parents would find his work in the library and enjoy it even if they didn't know who wrote it.

Tom currently resides in Ohio and North Carolina.